SEDUCTION THEORY

STORIES BY

THOMAS BELLER

W · W · NORTON & COMPANY · NEW YORK · LONDON

GRATEFUL ACKNOWLEDGMENT is made to the periodicals in which some of these stories first appeared: "Tearing at the Grapes" in *Mademoiselle;* "The Dark Piano" in *Southwest Review;* "The Hot Dog War" in *Epoch;* "Nondestructive Testing" in *Ploughshores*; and "A Different Kind of Imperfection" and "Live Wires" in *The New Yorker*. "A Different Kind of Imperfection" also appeared in *Best American Short Stories 1992*, Robert Stone, guest editor.

FIRST EDITION

THE TEXT *of this book is composed in Galliard with the display type set in News Gothic. Composition and manufacturing by the Maple-Vail Book Manufacturing Group. Book design by Marjorie J. Flock.*

Library of Congress Cataloging-in-Publication Data

Beller, Thomas.
    Seduction theory: stories / by Thomas Beller.
       p.   cm.
    I. Title.
PS3552.E53364S4   1995
813'.54—dc20   94-36704

ISBN 0-393-03767-3

W. W. Norton & Company, Inc., 500 Fifth Avenue, New York, N.Y. 10110
W. W. Norton & Company Ltd., 10 Coptic Street, London WC1A 1PU

1 2 3 4 5 6 7 8 9 0

For My Mother

The fact is always obvious much too late,
but the most singular difference between
happiness and joy is that happiness is a solid
and joy a liquid.

J. D. SALINGER

CONTENTS

Tearing at the Grapes   13

Deep Purple   27

Life Under Optimum Conditions   42

The Dark Piano   65

The Hot Dog War   85

World Without Mothers   100

Nondestructive Testing   118

A Different Kind of Imperfection   143

Seduction Theory   159

Live Wires   188

SEDUCTION THEORY

TEARING AT THE GRAPES

PAUL STOOD in front of the bathroom mirror and catalogued the catastrophes in his life. The list included those that had occurred already as well as those he considered imminent. On the list of catastrophes already occurred went such items as: Being dumped by his girlfriend of two years just before college graduation and one day before his birthday. Walking in on his suddenly ex-girlfriend and another man on his birthday. Having his apartment broken into just a few days after he moved in, when making a life for himself in New York City was starting to seem possible. Finding out he'd lost a chance at a dream job when an editor couldn't reach him because his answering machine had been stolen. Getting his nose broken by a riot policeman's club on an adventure into Times Square on New Year's Eve. Breaking it again six months later while dancing at a nightclub. Breaking it again a week ago, in a bank, just shy of a year from the first time.

Under the heading of imminent catastrophes he placed: The unquestionable thinning of his hair. The recent discovery, explained by a sculptor whom he dated for a short while, that his head was pointy. The prospect of being a bald man with a pointy head and a crooked nose. The possibility of having to return to the waiting room of an employment agency and confess to a smug paper pusher that his career as an editor hadn't really worked out the way he had hoped and it was time to examine his marketable skills. The assessment by the paper pusher that he had no marketable skills. The likelihood—based on recent history, his own disintegrating self-esteem, and the continuing deterioration of his features—that he would never have another love affair.

He stared at himself in the mirror and let his eyes focus on the nose: long, slightly hooked, barely crooked, a little swollen. It is a flag, he thought, placed right in the middle of my face, announcing my deterioration. He stood there like this, palms on the edge of the sink, elbows locked, shoulders hunched, staring until his face began to seem like a foreign object, something completely detached from what was doing the perceiving. It was like saying "purple" over and over again until the word lost all its meaning, shape, and familiarity. "Purple," he said, just to try it out. "Purple, purple, purple," he went on and on and on, until he caught himself and abruptly left the bathroom. He had a dinner date with a woman named Sarah.

They had met through mutual friends, become close when they shared proximity to the dissolution of another couple's relationship ("He's very upset." "She's confused."), and then set off onto a series of dinners and light gossip. Once, when they were both drunk at a party, they had flirted a little, but never mentioned it afterward. In the last four months, they had hardly spoken.

It had started out innocuously, this dinner date with a friend; something that had been put off again and again so that when they finally sat down together, there was a sudden silence, as if they had just then remembered that there was nothing much to say.

And so, though he had promised himself that he wouldn't mention it, Paul immediately spat out the news: "I broke my nose again."

"Oh, that's terrible!" said Sarah and leaned over to inspect his face. "It doesn't look broken," she added.

"But it is," said Paul, and then went on to recount how it had happened the first time, down in Times Square, and the second, when someone was gesticulating wildly while dancing at a club, and then last week, when he walked into a glass door.

"A glass door?" said Sarah.

"Yes. I know it sounds strange," said Paul. "It is. It happened in a bank. They must have just washed the glass. I never realized that when I walk I lead with my nose. But there's some consolation. I've become good friends with my ear, nose, and throat man. His name is Dr. Peltz. Every time I see him he looks at me like he can't believe I'm back."

"I wouldn't have noticed if you hadn't told me."

"He's taking a paternal interest in me. He says I'm his best customer."

"Well," said Sarah, "at least he's someone you can trust." She tried to look sympathetic but was becoming depressed. For reasons she couldn't begin to understand, ailing people flocked to her. She hadn't seen this man in months, had never really been that good friends with him, and as soon as they sit down to face each other he begins to blurt out his infirmities. She had read somewhere that Flaubert felt he attracted madmen and animals. She attracted sick men with the need to talk about whatever was bothering them. As for animals, she owned a cat. In spite of their having been together over two years, it still regarded her with suspicion.

"I'm not even sure I can trust him," said Paul. "Every time I go into his office he closes the door and says, 'Do you mind if I smoke?' I say no, but I think it's funny that an ear, nose, and throat man smokes. He says, 'If you mind, just say so. I insist I don't mind, and he pulls out a pack of unfiltered cigarettes. Would you trust this man?"

"I don't know. It would depend on what he told me."

"He informed me that a little dent in my nose is no problem, because there is a popular myth among women that men with big noses have big cocks." Paul meant to go on and say he'd always thought it was big hands, but something in Sarah's expression made him stop short.

Her smooth, high forehead furrowed conspicuously. "Did he really use the word '*cocks*'?"

Somehow, it wasn't the response he had expected.

At the end of the evening, Paul walked Sarah home and kissed her goodbye on the cheek. He noticed a concerned expression come over her face. They were in front of her apartment building on a quiet, tree-lined street in the West Village, peppered with dry brown leaves that crunched when you stepped on them. They stood apart, and there was a moment of silence. Then she lunged forward and wrapped her arms around him. He stood there, very still, then put his arms around her. He let his hand fall lightly on her back, feeling the texture of her jacket and the firmness underneath.

"This isn't sexual," she said from somewhere around the middle of his chest.

"Oh," said Paul, who had been surprised by this move but not unpleasantly.

"What I mean," she continued, "is this isn't a romantic gesture. I just wanted you to hold me."

They stood together like this for some time. Paul pushed his nose, sensitive as it was, onto the top of her head and smelled her hair. She moved her hands around on his lower back and this nearly excited him. After a while Paul was reminded of the dances at camp, when the last song of the night was either "Stairway to Heaven" or "Freebird," and everybody slow-danced during the slow part and stood there hugging during the fast part. The coolest couples would actually make out. Not being that cool, the two of them just hugged.

"What about your nose?" Sarah asked after a while.

"My nose?" said Paul, who had drifted into a trance, smelling Sarah's hair and rocking, barely rocking, to the imaginary sound of wailing electric guitars.

"You're pressing your nose into my head. I thought it was broken," she said. Paul noticed just then the way she said everything very calmly, with a great deal of reserve.

"It doesn't hurt," he said, and then reflected on how, unlike camp, they both had a private space they could retreat to.

"Do you think I could come upstairs?" he ventured, pulling his face back but keeping his arms hanging loosely on her hips. He was struck by the narrow bridge of her nose and the thin, tight curve of her lips, and how iridescent her skin looked in the pool of lamplight that surrounded them on the street. Her gray-blue eyes were curious, yet distant. Her face was that of a serious child.

"I don't think it's a good idea," she said.

"You don't?"

"No." She was suddenly very stern.

Once, in a similar situation, Paul had protested. He had argued something to the effect that it wasn't fair, that he didn't deserve to be treated this way; that what he actually deserved was sex. It had made everything worse. Since then, he had learned to be more patient. With that in mind, doing his best not to look dejected, he said, "Okay, I understand." He let his arms fall away and smiled weakly. She was looking even better. "I suppose I'll be seeing you," he continued, and started to take slow, leaden steps in the other direction.

Sarah was in a somber panic later that night. She felt impossibly cruel, and her cat, as if sensing her own self-doubt, was casting reproving looks at her and padding away whenever she came near. She lay sprawled on the only comfortable piece of furniture in the apartment, the bed. She reached over to the phone and dialed a friend.

"Hello?" the voice on the other end said, a little groggy because it was well past one in the morning. "Hello. Hello. Is anyone there?" Sarah listened to the voice, made certain associations, remembered certain things about the person attached to the voice, and, having made a connection of sorts, hung up.

She repeated this with several other friends. She didn't do it very often, make crank phone calls to friends, but she did it often enough so that she came to think that each person, after several "Hello, is anyone there?" sequences, secretly knew it was she. Then she started to feel offended because none of her friends wanted to talk to her, knowing it was she, behind the silence, desperately reaching out for human contact in the middle of the night. Finally a person said, "Sarah, is that you?"

"Yes," she said. Her voice was very soft and flat. Someone once commented that she used the same tone of voice for weddings and funerals. "What's the matter?" said the other voice, nearly as dispassionate as Sarah's.

"I can't fall asleep."

Silence.

"I can't . . . get laid."

"First of all, I wish you wouldn't use that language. It makes you sound desperate. And second of all, you're always getting laid." The other voice belonged to her older sister.

"I am desperate. I actually grabbed hold of a man this evening and wouldn't let go. I just stood there with my arms around him."

"What happened?"

"I told him to go away."

"I don't understand."

"He was injured."

"Everybody's injured."

"I was completely desolate and he seemed equally so, only sweeter. I wanted to be totally in love with him. Just for a minute. So I threw my arms around him, and while we were standing there I remembered that every man I get involved with who has these nagging ailments turns into torture. Why do men with physical problems flock to me?"

"It's because of our father. He spent at least an hour a day complaining about his asthma, his bursitis. What was the man's ailment, anyway?"

"He had a broken nose. He's apparently broken it a number of times, most recently last week."

"Is it big?"

"It seems a little swollen. Why?"

"You know what they say about noses."

"Oh stop it. His doctor said the same thing."

"All right. Fine. But next time call earlier. And Sarah, say something when I pick up the phone."

Paul was lying in bed, regretting the quote he used in his high school yearbook, when the phone rang. The quote was some Greek aphorism he had picked at random about choosing one's words carefully. Recently he had come to wish he had used something else and kept seeing great quotes in things he read. He had discussed this obsession with a friend, who suggested he was regressing.

"Hello," he said into the receiver and was met with silence. "Hello? Hel*lo*? Don't be afraid. I promise I won't tell a soul, whoever it is."

The phone was nearly back in the cradle when he thought he heard a voice. He put the phone back to his ear. "Hello? You can speak now. It's okay, really." He waited. There was a click on the other end.

The call distracted him from his yearbook regrets, and his thoughts began to drift over the arbitrary and haphazard images that had accumulated in his mind over the course of the day—a stringless violin lying in the street, the sidewalk flirtations between a tiny dachshund and a Great Dane, the conspicuously large supply of Peppermint Life Savers on display at his corner newsstand. The Life Savers, with their promise of a clean, minty taste and their suggestion of rescue, made him think of Sarah, whose skin, he imagined, might taste like peppermint. As much as he wanted to forget it, the awkward encounter he'd had with her had piqued his interest. He thought of it as an "experience."

His friend Walter thought differently. "I can't believe she did that to you!" he exclaimed.

"She didn't *do* anything to me," replied Paul. He remembered that it was agonizing to discuss women with Walter, who tended to have a rather unoptimistic outlook on the subject. "It sounds like she rejected you brutally," said Walter.

"She did not reject me! That's ridiculous! She made a pass at me and then chickened out. I could have slept with her if I had wanted to." These words horrified Paul, but he invariably slipped into this kind of tone with Walter, who seemed to request sexual arrogance from his friends.

"Do you want to?" Walter asked.

"Well, that's why I was calling." Walter and Sarah knew each other and shared some friends.

"You were calling so you could ask my opinion on whether to sleep with her?"

"Of course not. I mean, not specifically."

"Paul, I really can't go around advising people on whether to sleep together."

"I just wanted to know what you thought about it. You usually have penetrating insights into human relations."

"I don't have any 'penetrating insights' into you and Sarah."

"I wasn't asking you to be a fortune-teller," said Paul. "Tell me the most exotic thing about her that you know."

"I don't know anything exotic about her except that she

seems very reserved and goes out with men who seem to be constantly breaking their bones. I suppose that's exotic. I've seen her with an array of men in casts."

"I've broken my nose again."

"Again! This is becoming an occupation with you. How did it happen?"

"I don't want to talk about it."

"Well, I think it bodes well for you as far as Sarah is concerned."

"She doesn't know anything about it," said Paul, lying, and then added, a little timidly, "Do you think she's cute?"

Sarah was occasionally overtaken by a sense of collusion against her. The conspirators varied. Sometimes they were friends, sometimes they were strangers, like token booth clerks who wouldn't hurry when the train had just pulled into the station; sometimes it was her mother, sometimes her cat. In this instance, it was nature. Just as a slightly lonely sensation had begun to overtake her, nature dictated that all the leaves die and fall to the ground and that it become unbearably cold. She imagined she would be better off if she could schedule her periods of desperation for more optimistic earth cycles, like spring. But then there is always the business about April being the cruelest month. There really is no escape, she thought.

Again, the next night, Paul found himself talking into silence. "Hello . . ." he said, holding the receiver to his ear and waiting. A full minute went by.

"Hi," said a voice on the other end, announcing itself softly at just the moment that Paul was getting used to listening to a silent phone. "It's Sarah."

"I don't believe it," said Paul.

"You must think I'm rude."

"The word *original* comes to mind."

"Are you irritated that I'm calling you?"

"No, not exactly. But you're being very coy," he said.

"I was calling to apologize," she said.

"For what? The prank phone calls or the other night?"

She paused. "I didn't know there was anything to apologize for regarding the other night."

"Then why are you calling?"

"I wanted to talk to somebody."

"If you want to talk to somebody without saying anything, you should dial the weather. Calling people usually involves dialogue."

"I know, but I get nervous about contact with other people." She sounded a little distraught, and, for some reason, this gave Paul courage.

He imagined her slight naked body underneath the sheets, her round full hips tapering to her narrow waist, her back a little arched. He contemplated announcing that he was naked, but this sounded absurd. The very impulse to say this startled him. It made him feel ridiculous. And it would have been a lie anyway. He was in a distinctly unwashed pair of faded boxer shorts.

"How about if I come over," he said instead.

"It's two in the morning."

"I could take a cab."

"No, no. That's not why I called."

"I could be there in fifteen minutes."

"No! My God, what's the matter with you? Can't you talk to a woman without starting to froth?"

Paul had never thought of himself as the frothing type, but he didn't mind the idea. It was the sort of thing he would love to report to Walter.

"Listen," said Paul. "You've been making crank phone calls to me in the middle of the night and now we're having a conversation in the middle of the night about whether or not to speak when the person you called picks up the phone. Who's the frother here?"

"I was just calling because . . . I was worried about your nose," she said, and then added, "I just wanted to say hello."

"Can we have dinner again?"

"I don't know. I have nothing to say."

"That doesn't stop you from making phone calls," he said.

She arrived at the restaurant first and ordered a bottle of red wine. Paul came a little later, when she was already on her second glass. He had a few sips before they said a word. It was Paul who spoke first.

"We talked a lot more when we were less intimate," he said.

"Who says we're intimate now?"

They were silent again until the waiter came. They both ordered salads. It seemed appropriately temporary, given the situation. After they had sat sipping the wine for a while, Sarah spoke again.

"I'm sorry I made those phone calls. I only do it to people I feel close to."

"I'm privileged, I suppose."

"I hate all my old boyfriends."

"Are you trying to tell me let's just be friends?"

"As opposed to what?"

"As opposed to something more than friends."

"I thought we were friends," she said.

"We were, but we were descending friends. Now we're ascending something else." Paul liked the sound of it. The wine made him feel comfortable with the idea of systems and prescriptions and predictions.

He looked at her. Her eyes had that same cool appraising distance he had seen under the streetlamp. "It could be nice," he said, "the two of us."

She studied him for a moment, then looked away. "I don't know," she said. "I have an instinctive head-butting response to sex. I would break your nose immediately."

They sat in silence. Sarah thought about the line that she had just blurted out about how she hated all of her old boyfriends. She had said it half-jokingly, but the sound of it jarred her, and she considered whether or not it was true. She had been in love before, she was sure of that. And she had fallen out of love, she was sure of that, too. And, she decided, it wasn't the men she had gone out with that she hated, but rather this prospect of falling out of love, of things ending and dissolving. And now sitting across from her was this enthusiastic, attractive guy who seemed full of sweetness and greedy desire—things she liked in men—and yet something was holding her back, reminding her of how much easier it would be to stay away. And more than anything she hated herself for resisting on the grounds of playing it safe.

Paul, too, was thinking. Absentmindedly, he rearranged his silverware, possibilities turning over in his mind.

Here was this terribly cute girl whose skin shimmered like opal and who suddenly seemed like a dream to him, like the greatest thing, even considering that half the time she seemed completely out of her mind, with late-night phone calls, inexplicable mood swings, who knew what else. He tried to analyze why he liked her, but he couldn't put it into phrases. The fact that he had known her for a long time before he started liking her seemed odd. It made him wonder about how many other things were floating around on the periphery of his life, the subject of fleeting attention, that were destined to drift to center stage.

"Well, I like you," he said out of nowhere. He was going to add, "even though you're crazy," but stopped short, surprised at the degree of sincerity in his voice.

"I like you too," said Sarah, sighing, as if it was a fact of life she would have to live with.

Their hands found their way across the table and touched at the fingertips, then clasped. They sat forward on their elbows, looking across the table, scrutinizing each other for a change of heart.

DEEP PURPLE

ALEX FADER decided to take up the drums shortly after his tenth birthday. His inspiration was a boy named Seaton MacFall, a drummer, a friend, and, in only the narrowest definition of the phrase, a baby-sitter. Alex was a great admirer of Seaton, who was four years his senior. Seaton was thin and lanky (Alex was not) and possessed of what Alex thought was an almost magical assurance in moving through the world. Both Seaton and Alex lived in the "L" line of their building, Alex on the twelfth floor and Seaton on the sixth, but visiting Seaton's apartment was like visiting another planet, the land of the MacFalls: father, mother, sister, brother, all cheerful and upbeat, all with prominent cheekbones and bright blue eyes and faces exceptionally smooth and taut, as though their features had been spared the contortions of sadness and disappointment. The MacFalls' apartment was full of modern functional furniture, as opposed to Alex's, which was full of "antiques."

The apartment Alex lived in was occupied by himself and his mother. His father had exited the previous spring via a hospital room and cancer. It was a departure streaked with brief attempts at high spirits, like lines on a highway that blur together but don't quite connect. His father came home from the hospital for a brief period of time, during which an army of small dark bottles and glass vials sprang up beside his bed, only to return a few days later to the hospital, from which neither he nor the bottles returned. It was an unusually hot spring. A few days after the funeral, Alex had his tenth birthday, and then everything melted into a summer which Alex moved through as if in slow motion. Time, among other things, made less sense than it had before. He took walks around his apartment, whose atmosphere was hot and silent. In an odd way Alex enjoyed it—all that soundless air was like floating.

One afternoon in midsummer Alex tried to explain to his mother that the baby-sitter-baby-sittee dynamic between Seaton and himself had changed into a more conventional friendship.

"You don't have to pay Seaton anymore," he announced one day.

"I don't?" she said. "Why not? I thought you liked Seaton."

"I do. And he likes me. We're friends. That's why you don't have to pay him."

"I'm glad you're friends. But he's still your baby-sitter and I have to pay him. It doesn't mean he's not your friend also."

"But he's *just* my friend."

"I'm not saying you're not friends with Seaton. I'm just saying that he's also your baby-sitter."

"But Mom!" Alex's voice tightened with frustration. Then, as if it were the worst thing he could say, he blurted out: "Kids are people too!" Several months earlier he had been in the studio audience of a television show called *Wonderama,* whose theme song, which the whole audience sang in an exuberant chorus, went: "Kids are people, kids are people . . . Kids are people too! Wackadoo, Wackadoo, Wackadoo . . ." Since then this phrase had been the last resort for situations in which he felt his mother was being unjust.

Now, he studied her face for signs of hurt at his protest, but she only looked at him with a serene if slightly sorrowful expression. Deep down he knew that the jab he had delivered had nothing to do with the phrase "Kids are people too," but with the single word "Mom," which, with no warning, had replaced "Mama" after he returned home from the filming of the show.

"Now be sure to go home and tell your mom and dad what a good time you had!" the host said at the end of the day, and that night at bedtime Alex had said, "Good night, Mom," and the word "Mama" hadn't passed his lips since.

So Seaton continued to be a "baby-sitter," if only technically, and Alex continued to venture downstairs on weekend afternoons and some weekday evenings to spend time at his friend's house. Alex could never get used to how two identical spaces could have such different atmospheres, and in no room was this more true than in Seaton's, the same one Alex occupied six floors above.

The most striking difference was that while Alex's room was painted a polite shade of white, Seaton's was a dark shade of purple, in semigloss. He had painted it himself one weekend while his parents were away. As he explained it, they were somewhat startled to find his room purple when they returned but there wasn't much discussion about it. "Thing is," he said, "by then it was done. So what could they do, you know? What's the point of getting upset?"

Against this purple background Seaton had mounted numerous posters of his favorite rock and roll bands. They sometimes played a game in which Alex would point to one of the posters and Seaton would take out the band's records and play them on his stereo, telling him which songs were his favorite and giving certain historical facts about the group. Alex thought it was a neat coincidence that Seaton's favorite group was a band called Deep Purple.

The most intriguing element of Seaton's room, however, was the drum set that sat in the corner. Alex regarded it warily, as if it were some special machine that, if used properly, might take flight at any moment.

For a long time Seaton refused to play the drums in front of Alex, saying something about the neighbors complaining if he didn't keep to his schedule. One day, though, while Seaton was playing a Deep Purple record, he got very excited about something. "Hear that? Do hear the double time he's doing?" He jumped up and started to play along with the record. The room changed then. It filled up with a sound so large that no other sound was left in it, not even the stereo. Seaton's body became like an engine with pistons all moving at different speeds. He played a pattern that repeated itself, a complicated beat, and the repetition of this pattern at such a loud volume had a hypnotic effect on Alex. His stomach rose inside his body. He felt as if he had just reached the top of a roller coaster ride and was in the midst of its first terrifying descent.

Then Seaton stopped, neatly laying his sticks down like utensils at the end of a modest dinner.

"See what I mean?" he said to Alex. "He does that double time on the snare in the middle of the song, you know? It really rocks."

That evening Alex asked his mother for a drum set. The request took her by surprise. Alex knew instinctively that Seaton's room, with its purple walls and posters of rock bands, would not be the kind if thing to inspire her to action, so he paused after his initial request and then added, "It's the musical instrument I'm most interested in." He sensed that the word "interests" had a special authority.

"A drum set?" she said.

"Yeah. Like Seaton's. Can I?" He watched her face closely to see how she was reacting. He had been engaged in a slow set of experiments as to how far he could influence his mother. He didn't realize the extent to which this was possible until one hot summer morning, just a month after his father's funeral, when he looked up from the sports page he had been studying while eating a bowl of cereal and said, "Let's go to a baseball game."

There was a long silence. His mother was not a sports fan. "A baseball game?" she said at last. "Oh no. We couldn't do that." He returned to his bowl of cereal and the paper beneath it.

A minute later she said, "Yes! What a lovely idea. When can we go?"

There was a game out at Shea Stadium that day, and they arrived in the second inning. They hurried up the dark narrow ramp arm in arm, clutching their tickets as the din of the stadium approached. Just as they got to the top of the ramp the crowd let out a roar—it was as if they had entered the insides of a giant cacophonous tulip, a blast of color and sound; they had arrived just in time to see a player from the visiting team tagged out at the plate.

They spent the afternoon sitting happily in their seats, he explaining what was happening without moving his eyes from the field and she watching him watch, happy for the distraction. That summer was the flavor of hot dogs; the sensation of the thin wrap of plastic that stretched over the tops of sodas being peeled slightly back to allow for a sip; the sound of the rumbling wheels of the 7 train winding its way through Queens, majestically perched above a sea of two-story row houses.

But most important for Alex, that was the summer when he was right! He had an idea and by merely by stating it out loud he had altered the course of events in his life. This was a new development. The events of the world had been speeding along according to their own inscrutable logic, but now the possibility of influencing them had arisen. Suddenly his own home became a place where he could control his destiny.

Now, he focused his eyes on his mother. "Please?" he said, inflecting the word with as much tremulousness as possible so as to reassure her that he was at her mercy. "I want to be a drummer and I can't be a drummer without a drum set."

"I'll think about it," she said.

A few days later she reached a verdict. "If you want a drum set you'll have to take lessons. If you stay with the lessons we'll see what comes next."

"But Mom!" Said Alex. "I want a drum set now!"

"Well, if you really want one, then you'll work hard at your lessons and perhaps you'll get one. You'll have something to look forward to."

This phrase, "You'll have something to look forward to," was the single most infuriating formulation his mother regularly used to thwart his wishes. Hearing it had become synonymous with being unhappy.

The music school was on Eightieth Street and Broadway, above Woolworth's. His teacher was named Mr. Frick, a bored-looking man whose face was frozen in a state of perpetual apprehension, as though he was constantly expecting whomever he was with to break out into tears. On his first day Alex was handed a small drum pad the size of a salad dish. "This is called a practice pad," said Mr. Frick. "It's what you are going to use to learn to play the drums." He didn't sound optimistic.

Alex looked at the practice pad with despair. "Don't I get to play on a drum set?" he said.

"First you'll learn on this. That'll keep you busy for a while." Then he produced a book of sheet music and added, "And you're going to learn to read this."

Alex looked at Mr. Frick and then at the sheet music and a sudden fatigue overtook him; it was similar to what he felt while sitting in his dentist's waiting room, anticipating a cavity. There was no sheet music in Seaton's room, he thought. Sheet music had all the wrong associations. It reminded him of the polite ribbons of melody that flowed from the living-room piano when his mother played. He didn't want ribbons. He wanted rocks, huge boulders of sound, and on the sheet music before him lay a mound of pebbles.

But Alex enjoyed the lessons. He was taught how to hold the sticks, and then how to hit the practice pad in such a way that the small, teardrop-shaped tip bounced several times in quick succession. After a while he could get both sticks to do it one after the other, making a sustained sound. "You're getting the hang of it," said Mr. Frick in the well-rehearsed tone of cautious encouragement. By the second lesson Alex decided that Mr. Frick wasn't a tyrant, and by the third he decided that he was faintly likable in the way a peanut is likable. Years of being cloistered in a small room with youngsters earnestly performing inept drum rolls had given Mr. Frick a slightly crazed quality that Alex enjoyed. Mr. Frick's shiny head was covered by a few strands of short hair which began each lesson in neatly combed formation and then proceeded to slowly rise up, so that by the end of the lesson it was as if a fleet of submarines had surfaced on Mr. Frick's head, their periscopes peering in various directions. He tried to imagine Mr. Frick as a kid and decided he must have been the sort of kid who was quiet and withdrawn but who occasionally surprised everyone by smashing a birthday cake in his own face.

The summer faded into fall, fifth grade began, and the drum lessons continued, as did his visits with Seaton. One day Alex arrived downstairs and discovered that Seaton had shaved his head and dyed the remaining stubble bright pink. Alex eyed him suspiciously. "My girlfriend dared me to do it," Seaton explained nonchalantly as they walked down the long corridor from the foyer to his room. "She wanted to see if I loved her enough to do something wild."

This seemed like an extremely reasonable explanation. They entered the purple room.

Besides the shocking-pink hair, there had been other changes in Seaton in recent months, small things that Alex couldn't quite put his finger on but could sense. For the most part, Alex thought these changes were for the better. Seaton no longer used the word "baby-sit," or acted as if spending time with Alex was a job in any way. He treated Alex like a normal person, not like a kid. The two of them spent hours languishing in Seaton's purple room, listening to records and talking while Alex eyed the drum set sitting dormantly in the corner. Seaton would recount various encounters with girls or with beer, and Alex would nod casually as though he had done it all as well.

Seaton, however, never let Alex play the drums. But now, as they walked into the room, Seaton said: "You can play them if you want. We changed my schedule and I'm allowed to play for the next half hour." He collapsed into the big red leaky beanbag that was situated next to the stereo. Alex was shocked by this sudden generosity; its complete unpredictability had a logic that elevated Seaton far above the other grown-ups he knew.

Alex went over to the drums, sat on the stool, and prepared to begin a drumroll on the snare drum. He anticipated the same smooth purring sound that he produced on his practice pad. But it was different. Alex felt a dense sheet of sound spring up and envelop the room; it was like sheets of rain beating down on a tin roof. He continued the slight, almost imperceptible movement of his wrists and fingers controlling the sticks, and felt like a magician who was making an object rise into the air and hover.

Later they went outside to Riverside Park to play catch with a football. It was late afternoon and the light was a powdery blue that seemed to come from no particular place. Some people stared at Seaton's hair, but Alex felt invincible walking next to him. He was always a little nervous about the park due to a gang of kids that occasionally ran up to him and called him fat.

But this never happened when Seaton was around. And now in addition to Seaton, there was an invisible white sheet of sound wrapped around him, like a cloak.

"Excuse me, Mr. Frick," said Alex at the start of his next lesson, "but why do I have to deal with this sheet music stuff? Why can't I just play on a drum set? I already have, you know, at my friend's house."

"All the great drummers read sheet music," said Mr. Frick.

"I don't want to be like all the great drummers," said Alex. "I want to rock."

Mr. Frick gave Alex a long fatigued stare and then flipped open the book of sheet music.

"Look," said Alex, "if you had to guess, when do you think I could get a drum set? Soon?"

"That's up to your mother," said Mr. Frick.

"But you could have some influence."

"It's my business to teach you the elementary skills of the drums. We have a long way to go with that."

Alex stared at Mr. Frick and decided he was receiving instruction from a hard-boiled egg.

Alex told Seaton about his exasperation with Mr. Frick as they sat in Seaton's purple room and listened to records. Seaton didn't approve of Mr. Frick. "That guy sounds like an idiot," he said. "What you really need is to just get into it. You can't get into it with sheet music, a practice pad, and an old fart sitting next to you."

"Yeah!" said Alex defiantly. He was very in love with Seaton just then. Seaton, it seemed, was the only person on earth who saw things as they were—Mr. Frick was an old fart; Alex was a grown-up.

"Check this out," said Seaton, putting an album on the turntable. "It'll blow your mind."

The record began to play, and Alex listened intently. The words had something to do with ground control trying to speak to Major someone, and the music didn't seem particularly rocking, but he nodded his head to the beat as Seaton was doing.

Next to him Seaton sat in his beanbag rolling what appeared to be a cigarette. When he was finished he looked up and saw Alex staring at him. "Hey Alex," he said. "You smoke pot?"

"Yeah," said Alex reflexively.

"Sure you do," said Seaton. His eyebrow swerved upward with meaningful sarcasm. "You want to try some?" Now he flicked both eyebrows up and down quickly. Seaton's manner just then seemed very in keeping with the sense of conspiratorial fun that permeated all of the MacFall family. When Alex once asked Mr. MacFall what he did he replied, "I'm an electrician!" Mr. MacFall always wore crisp charcoal-gray suits and his silver hair was slicked back neatly over his head.

Alex had hesitated and then asked, "Is it fun?"

Mr. MacFall replied with a burst of laughter.

Now Seaton seemed to have that same kind of expression on his face; it was cruel and friendly at the same time. He reached into his pocket and took out a lighter, put the lumpy cigarette between his lips, and held the flame to it. He puffed deeply and then held it up for inspection while he held his breath. When he exhaled, the room filled up with a rich sweet odor that Alex could taste in his mouth. "Here," said Seaton, and held the smoking object out towards Alex.

"What is it?" said Alex.

"It's a joint, you idiot," he said, and smiled after he said it, which softened the words. "Usually you don't get high the first time, but this is supposed to be really good stuff."

Alex guided it to his lips, squinting.

"That's right," said Seaton. "Now inhale and hold your breath."

Alex had extensive experience holding his breath, having spent countless hours practicing in his bathtub, but this was different. After a few seconds he exhaled a huge cloud of smoke accompanied by several scalding staccato coughs that made his eyes water. Seaton seemed to find this very amusing and laughed. Alex smiled too through his subsiding spasm of coughs. They passed the joint back and forth, and Alex managed to avoid coughing. When it was almost gone there was a knock on the door. The knock startled them both.

"Oh shit!" said Seaton. He frantically stubbed out the joint with one hand while gathering the lighter and ashtray with the other. The music was still blaring loudly.

"Seaton?" came the voice on the other side of the door. It was the cheerful voice of Mrs. MacFall. Alex could picture the inquisitive smile on her face, her head slightly tilted and her chin angled upward in expectation of a reply.

"Yeah?" said Seaton, trying to sound calm. He turned down the stereo.

"Seaton, can I come in?"

"No!" Seaton shouted hoarsely. His voice was full of panic, and, sensing this, he composed himself for his next line. "I can't talk right now. I'm baby-sitting Alex. I'll be out in a little while."

Alex received the news that he was being baby-sat like a

lottery winner who's told that there's been a mistake and he didn't win after all. He sat amidst the purple walls, the drums hovering in the corner, and felt a slight tilting sensation to go with the strange taste in his mouth. Neither of them said a word for several minutes.

"Wow," said Seaton eventually. "That was close." Then he turned towards Alex and smiled the same happy sinister smile he had before. "Are you stoned?"

Later, Alex took the elevator up six flights and stepped out on the landing with the small tentative steps of an astronaut. He stared at the front door to his apartment for a long time and then paused with his hand on the doorknob, feeling its cool brass shape fit smoothly into the palm of his hand.

It was shortly after that close call, however, that Seaton suddenly disappeared. His absence wasn't explained to Alex right away, but eventually his mother sat him down and said that Seaton's parents thought that he could do with a change in environment and he had gone off to boarding school.

"But the semester isn't over," said Alex. "Why would he need a change of environment in the middle of the semester?"

Alex's mother couldn't answer this one, so she changed the subject.

"How are the drum lessons?" she said.

"Boring," said Alex. "Do you think I can get a drum set soon?"

"We'll see," said his mother.

"Why did they send him to boarding school?" he asked with the agitation of a lawyer who knows the case has already been lost.

"I don't know," said his mother. "I suppose they thought it would make him happier."

Alex contemplated this for a moment. Here was another unannounced departure, inexplicable and, it seemed, irrevocable. Alex considered Seaton's sudden absence and felt the sinking feeling that came over him when the events in his life slid beyond the narrow realm of his control, out into the cold blue atmosphere where they spent most of their time happening and happening and happening, immune to reason or special pleading.

The next day Alex arrived in his lobby just as the elevator door was about to close. His arm shot out and stabbed the button, and he watched gleefully as the door halted and withdrew, like a curtain. There stood Mr. MacFall, the electrician, in his charcoal-gray pinstripe suit. Alex stepped in and the elevator door enclosed them in the small dimly lit box with fake wood panels. They started to rise.

"Hello, Alex," said Mr. MacFall. He was cheerful in the assertive way adults were when they wanted to keep things brief.

"Hi," he responded meekly. They passed the second floor.

"How are you?" said Mr. MacFall. They passed the third floor. Alex was seized with a sudden sense of urgency.

"Where's Seaton?" he said.

Mr. MacFall's face kept its pleasant expression. "Oh, he's up in Vermont. Boarding school. Seaton wanted a little change of scenery." They passed the fourth floor.

"Why did he want a change of scenery?"

"Well, sometimes it's a good idea to get away from where you've been and go somewhere new. Seaton wanted to go somewhere new."

A little window of light that was the fifth-floor landing flickered by in the elevator window.

Alex was about to ask why Seaton wanted to go somewhere new, but he realized time was running out, so he asked a more pressing question instead. "What are you going to do with his room? The purple walls and everything."

Mr. MacFall's smile didn't waver exactly, but the corners of his eyes seemed to narrow momentarily, as if a spotlight had been raked across his face. The elevator slowed to a stop on the sixth floor.

"We're going to paint it," he said. The elevator churned and the door slid open. Mr. MacFall stepped out onto the landing with a polite nod, his smile intact. "Goodbye, Alex," he said.

LIFE UNDER OPTIMUM CONDITIONS

IT WAS A SATURDAY. Michael and Jane tossed and turned in bed all morning while strange unidentifiable music wafted in through the window of her apartment. At noon they went outside and discovered a street fair getting underway on Greenwich Avenue. It was a good day for a fair; it was autumn, and the light was unobstructed by clouds or heat. The people milling around beneath the sky's overwhelming blue seemed subdued and small, like movie extras wandering around a set waiting for instructions.

They quickly identified the source of their restless morning as a trio of enthusiastic South American Indians who were producing cheerful, flute-oriented sounds with ancient-looking instruments. Michael recognized them as regulars at the Times Square subway platform. They seemed much happier to be in the sun.

"I wonder what kind of music they're playing?" said Jane.

"Peruvian love ritual music," said Michael.

"What's a Peruvian love ritual?"

"I'll show you sometime," he said.

Jane and Michael had been together only three months, but

it seemed like longer to both of them; it was hard for each to imagine what life had been like without the other. As soon as they made a connection, both emotionally and sexually, they both clutched at it without hesitation or deliberation, and the mutuality of their clutching had brought them even closer. It had been a long time since either had been involved in anything approximating love.

That was three months ago. It hadn't dissipated, the excitement, but it had leveled.

Jane looked over at Michael as they strolled through the fair. His eyes lingered over tables strewn with jewelry, dormant pots of hot oil waiting for their first falafel ball, other women as they walked past. This lingering annoyed her, though she wasn't sure if it was the lingering itself or the fact that he wasn't more careful to hide it from her.

She examined the scene before her. Everything seemed exposed and wrong in this harsh bright light, which seemed designed for a more pastoral setting.

"Do you want anything for breakfast?" he said distractedly.

"Cotton candy," she said.

As they strolled through the fair Jane looked at the faces of the vendors standing patiently in their booths. She imagined that they were trying to look calm in anticipation of the afternoon rush, which they had no guarantee would come. There was a subtext of panic in the air, she thought. The whole scene seemed like one of those disaster movies that start with an ordinary situation which then is suddenly disrupted by a natural catastrophe during which the hero and heroine are separated, and they then spend the rest of the movie trying to find each other amid the hysterical, wounded population. And here was Michael with this newfound propensity for looking at other women. Maybe it was one of those movies in which the hero falls in love with the nurse who tends to his injured forehead. She had a brief pang of hatred for the nurse and then for Michael. She desired a drastic change of scenery.

"Let's do something strange," she said.

"You mean sexually?" he asked.

"No, not in that way. I meant something unusual. We could go to the zoo, for example."

He considered it. Seals, elephants. He thought of the dirty white polar bears moping around a small cave, crouched on a protruding rock. He thought of taxidermy.

"I don't know," he said. "I don't know if the zoo is what today is all about."

She looked at him surreptitiously. His eyes continued to wander, indifferent yet interested. The combination of detachment and engagement in his expression had been one of the first things she had noticed about him, and it attracted her. It made him very hard to read. It was a quality, she later discovered, that had an opposite, when he became an open book, hiding nothing, disclosing everything, and then abruptly slamming shut. These bouts of full disclosure surprised her at first, and continued to surprise her, because she never knew when they would come, and she couldn't seem to provoke them. Now, however, his initial mystery lingered. Something to do with his smile.

On the first night they met, talking at a party, Michael had known immediately he liked her; even after just a few minutes, he had thought that in some way he already knew her. But the closer he got to her the more elusive she became. This had dawned on him one night while they were lying in bed after having had the kind of sex after which it seems that there is no real reason to leave that particular bed ever again. They had already begun the process of talking about their sexual biographies, telling each other about past lovers, and she was in the midst of describing her first date with the last man she had been with before Michael. "Boyfriend," she said, was too glorious a term for him.

"He said, 'See, watch this,' and he cupped my face with his hand, under the chin"—she demonstrated with her own hand—"and he turned my whole face very authoritatively toward his and held it there, like he was inspecting a small antique. Then he said, 'Women love this. If a woman lets me do that to her, hold her face like this, I know I can sleep with her. Even if she knows it's a manipulative, obvious thing to do. They'll sleep with me anyway, just like you will.' "

His body tensed a little as she told this story, partly in amazement at the arrogance of this man, partly in horror that she had been with him at all. Externally he wanted to hear her say that she had denounced him as a deluded idiot, yet he felt something else inside of him poise expectantly as he asked his question: "And did you sleep with him then?"

"Yes," she said. "He was very good-looking," she added, as though an explanation was needed.

"That same night?"

"Yes, I think so."

"He not only did this preposterous move, but he actually drew attention to it as a move and then you slept with him just like he said you would? I can't believe that. Were you turned on by that at all? The arrogance?"

"A little," she said.

He paused for a moment, as if examining a small cut. "What else did you do with him? Sexually, I mean."

She shivered slightly and moved closer to him, not answering. For a moment he hated her, was completely disgusted with her, but then that changed into something different. It was confusing.

"In some way," he said after a moment, "I sort of wish I could be that way, confident and removed. But I can't. I thrive on wimpiness and confession."

"Confess something," she said now, lying next to him.

"Anything?"

"No. Confess the sort of thing that you think a calculated self-assured man would never confess to a woman he wanted to sleep with. Tell me something totally self-defeating."

It took a minute.

"I love you," he said.

Jane was a sound editor for movies. She worked freelance and sporadically, but she was good at it and made quite a bit of money when she worked. It was a peculiar sort of vocation, the kind that appears more interesting than it is, or at least that's how she thought of it. She wanted to make movies of her own, but that ambition had been put on hold for a while.

Michael wanted to be a filmmaker also, and had taken the arduous rout that begins with the title "Production Assistant," a job which in his case entailed running around making sure everyone had enough doughnuts and coffee in their trailers. Eventually he managed to work his way into a job as an assistant to the key grip on one movie. "If the cinematographer is in charge of the light," he explained to a friend in a fit of enthusiasm, "The key grip is charge of the shadows." The speed of his ascent wasn't as fast as he had hoped, however, and though he wasn't despondent, the possibility of being the next Orson Welles had more or less come and gone. Jane was two years older than Michael, and, in the ecosystem of the film business, much more accomplished. Neither of these facts came between them, though they were vaguely acknowledged.

Jane's inspiration about how to make the day right came in the form of a rented car and a scenic lodge upstate. She offered to pay for the trip. It was her idea, and after all, she rationalized, she was older.

By the time they were on the highway it was midafternoon. He drove. The sun retained the sharp aggressive quality it had earlier but seemed more appropriate in the context of a wide-open space. It cheered Jane up. After less than an hour of driving north the leaves began to take on brilliant hues of yellow, red, and orange. The colors outside calmed her nerves, which had inexplicably flared earlier that day. She thought disapprovingly that she might have been having a boring and completely unreasonable attack of possessiveness.

The idea that a meandering glance of Michael's could have that effect bothered her tremendously. But what bothered her more insidiously was the thought that her sudden attack of irritability might have been just an outward symptom of a deeper dissonance with the way things were between the two of them, a dissatisfaction that didn't so much have to do with Michael himself as with the very nature of their union, the predictability of it.

They were headed towards a place called the Beekman Arms. She had never been there, but a friend of hers had once had a very romantic weekend there and that was recommendation enough. The friend described lavish rooms with lace-fringed linen, a four-poster bed, a fireplace. The thought of the posts intrigued her. She imagined herself naked, with a limb tied to each post, the street-fair patrons drifting by disinterestedly, gazing casually down at the display. Michael was among them. He wouldn't just stand over her like the rest of them did, he would untie her right away. She thought so, anyway.

When Michael first met Jane, he had liked her because she seemed strong. It was the kind of strength that is a mixture of certainty and caution. But recently he had begun to see a peculiar apprehensiveness creep into her body language. In the car, her facial expression took on a nervously relieved quality, as if she had just found her seat at a baseball game after a long period of being lost. He sensed that she was exposing herself somehow, that an invitation was being made, however subtle, and it was up to him to respond to it appropriately. As to what kind of response was appropriate, he had no idea; but he wasn't without his hunches.

He thought about the story she had told of the awful man who had held her face and announced she would sleep with him. That relationship had lasted only a few months, and even though it was she who ended it, Michael had the sense that the man's detachment had been a source of his attraction. Michael wondered if Jane wanted him to be the arrogant non-boyfriend, if she would be disappointed if he didn't start being cold and commanding.

The flaming scenery flew past him while he tried to think of how to go about this. Finally he blurted out, "I want you to give me a blow job right now." It sounded a little strained but, he thought, it was a start.

She turned her head and faced him without moving any other part of her body. There was a slight crease between her eyebrows. She didn't even look perplexed, which would have been bad enough. She looked slightly scolding, as if he had spilled chocolate pudding on a shirt she had specifically instructed him to keep clean.

"What?" she said softly, with a slight amount of incredulity.

In spite of her devastating facial expression he made a split-second decision to persevere, perseverance being part of the kind of masculinity he was shooting for. "I want you to reach over, unzip my pants, take my cock out, put it in your mouth, and suck on it until I come." He paused for a moment and then added, "Now." The last word, however, came out with less authority than he would have liked. He thought he saw her roll her eyes as she turned back to face the road, hands crossed on her lap. He focused on the road and tried to engross himself deeply in the act of driving.

"I'm looking at the scenery," she said finally.

They drove on in silence.

Jane was disgusted. This sudden and completely uncharacteristic outburst on Michael's part was not what this trip was supposed to be about. It was supposed to be a time of sensitizing and repose. Something nice. Instead she had been assaulted by a flasher in the confines of her own rented car, and she was now supposed to have dinner and presumably sleep with this same deluded adolescent. The possibilities for romance suddenly seemed very bleak. She scanned his face out of the corner of her eye, but all she could perceive was a moronic two-handed concentration on the shadow-dappled road. It wasn't like the

49

suggestion itself was so awful; she probably would have done it if he had at least attempted to be seductive.

What had started as a wonderful adventure full of romantic possibilities had suddenly become something entirely different. Earlier during the ride the crisp autumn air and unfiltered sunlight had made her think of chestnuts, the smell of burning leaves, and warm cuddling under a thick down comforter. Now it evoked memories of old smelly pencils and Halloween. That particular holiday—only a week away—had once been her favorite, but recently it had taken on an ominous quality, particularly starting the previous year.

She had just moved into a new apartment and had asked the neighbors if children with bags would be coming by. They said yes, a few. She dutifully went out and bought nice candies in small quantities. In the early part of the evening she anticipated the arrival of the small bag bearers with some dread, resenting the imposition. But after a little while she started to enjoy the idea and turned off the lights to create a heightened effect in her apartment; she even regretted not buying a plastic jack-o-lantern to put the candies in. The night wore on and she sat in the dark listening to her radio. Not a single child came by. At the time she just thought it was eerie, but the next morning she woke feeling like she had suffered a personal rejection.

They pulled into the Beekman Arms parking lot. The first thing she saw was an abnormally large and glowering pumpkin leering out at her from the office window. The expression carved on its face was like that of an obnoxious man who had just seen down her shirt after she bent to pick something up.

"Well," said Michael, his voice raspy from not having spoken in a while, "we're here." He was trying to sound cheerful.

Repenting, she thought. How pathetic.

"Yes, it would appear that way," she said.

They went inside and she registered while he watched. A bellman took them to their room, opening the door for them and turning on the lights. Inside was a four-poster bed, a couch, a fireplace, an elegant glass bottle filled with brandy on the mantel, two snifters by its side. There was plush brown carpet.

It looked seedy and illicit, she thought. She walked into the bathroom without saying a word, and stared at herself glumly in the mirror, looking at the tiny crow's-feet developing around her eyes.

Michael surveyed the room. The bedroom seemed like a sexual obstacle course. It was brimming with possibilities, starting with the fact that it was an empty hotel room at his disposal, and embellished by the couch, the carpet, and especially the grand and voluptuous bed: everything about the place seemed to expect sexual athleticism and experimentation. The room was a blank sheet of paper inviting him to scribble on it, but he had forgotten his crayon. While Jane was in the bathroom he sat gloomily on the edge of the bed and stared at the logs in the dark lifeless fireplace.

They went to dinner in silence. The Beekman Arms restaurant, highly recommended, was suffused in warm atmosphere and busy cheer. It smelled like baked apples and steak. George Washington had once stayed there apparently, on his way to somewhere else. The enormous front door creaked open slowly and smoothly when he pulled on its latch, letting Jane in first.

When they were seated he ordered a bottle of wine after glancing over the wine list, his eyes sticking to the thin column of numbers on the right, since the wider columns of names and dates next to it meant nothing to him. He ordered the second-cheapest one.

Jane was looking around the room. Everyone, she thought, seemed in good spirits. There were happy families, suave middle-aged couples up from the city, and some slightly more earthy types in plaid or flannel of some kind who lived in the area and were pleased to be casually exuding authenticity amidst all these tourists. And there were quite a few lovers, all of whom, she imagined, must be happier than they were just then.

"Do you think you would ever like to live somewhere besides New York?" he asked. "Like in the country?"

"I feel that way nearly all the time," she said.

"Being here makes me feel that way. There's something about the air . . ." He trailed off because she gave him a funny look. "What?" he said.

"Nothing," she replied, looking at the menu.

"Do you think I'm being silly by making dumb small talk?"

She shrugged.

"It is a little ridiculous. I mean, it's not what we usually talk about. But then again we don't usually drive into the country and stay at a hotel."

"Do you want to go back?" she said.

"No! God no." He seemed genuinely alarmed at the idea. "It's just weird."

"Well," she said, "if you think about it there are a lot of things we haven't done together. For all the time we've spent together we still don't really know each other that well."

He thought about this for a moment, a little hurt. "I think we know each other pretty well. Unless there are some deep dark secrets you haven't told me about." She didn't reply. "Are there any deep dark secrets you haven't told me about?"

"I don't know," she said casually, while inspecting the menu. "Probably. Do you have any you haven't told me about?" She didn't look up while asking the question; that would have implied too much interest in the answer.

"I don't know," he said. "Probably."

The wine arrived. Michael knew nothing about wine except for the particular ritual of tasting it when it arrived, which he had observed his father do many times. The waiter poured a little into his glass and Michael commenced his act: after swirling it in his glass, sniffing it, and sipping it pensively with his chin slightly raised, he turned to the waiter and gave a polite nod. As the waiter poured their wine it occurred to Michael for the first time that it might have been an act for his father also. The thought displeased him immensely.

Without their having to say anything specific, their manner softened towards each other over the course of dinner, and by the time they made their way back to their room they were holding hands. After one glass of wine, Michael had decided the situation called for something stronger and he began to drink scotch, saying that the advent of the cooler weather was perfect scotch season. He had several. She finished the wine by herself. So the walk to the room was a little unsteady. And in spite of everything, they made love, or at least engaged in something similar.

The event lived up to his greatest fears: everything seemed a little forced, a little unnatural. The room itself—its props and its atmosphere and its ghosts of past good sex—seemed to goad him into all kinds of unlikely things.

She was amused at this unexpected burst of energy and went along with it, a little puzzled. It became a sexual scavenger hunt: do it lying on the bed, do it with her sitting on the bed while he stood on the floor, do it on the floor next to the fireplace (unlit), and do it in a particularly athletic position halfway between the couch and floor. Then the flower pot on the coffee table got knocked over and spilled on the carpet and he started to feel silly. What was left of his erection went away and she said, trying not to sound too discouraging, "Why are we doing this?" and he said, "I don't know," and laughed.

They lit the fire and got under the covers with the lights out.

She could feel his body breathing next to hers. They weren't intentionally not touching, but they weren't embracing either. The fire gave the room a nice flickering atmosphere. The sheets were cold but warming fast.

"Michael," she said softly, her voice flickering like the fire.

"Yeah?"

"When you said you had some deep dark secrets that I didn't know about, what were they?"

"I didn't say I had any. I said I might. And besides, it was in reply to you. You said you might have some deep dark secrets that I don't know about. Do you?"

"I don't know. It depends what a deep dark secret is."

"Something I don't know about, I suppose."

"You don't know that I sucked my thumb until I was ten years old, but that's not what I would call a deep dark secret."

"That's true," he said. "But it's cute."

"It's got to be something that could potentially affect the way the other person sees them. The sort of thing that if someone confronted you with it, you might lie."

He was silent for a while. "Do you have something like that? A secret like that?"

"Maybe," she said.

"What is it?"

"I said maybe." They were quiet again. "If I tell you a secret like that, will you tell me one?" she said.

He didn't answer right away. She turned on her side and tried to read his expression, but his head was turned towards the fire. "All right," he said.

She cuddled next to him and put her head on his shoulder, as if preparing to hear a story instead of tell one.

"You go first," he said.

"Why me? You start."

"It was your idea. You suggested it."

She considered her options. There was a time that a good deal of what she had done sexually would have seemed slightly scandalous. But that was before she had done it. Now it didn't seem like much. There was one tawdry, slightly gross thing that she could report. It really and truly was something she didn't like to think about and hardly ever did. But, she supposed, that was precisely the kind of thing she was supposed to provide, so she launched in.

"This is something gross and I'm going to make it short. It isn't the end of the world. I don't think you'll jump out of bed or anything, but it's sufficiently unpleasant."

"There's no need to rush it," he said.

"Oh, it's sleazy enough. I'm sure you'll enjoy it. It happened when I was a junior in high school. Junior year in high school was not a great year for me for a variety of reasons. Anyway, I had a crush on this man. It was just a schoolgirl crush, but anyway."

"A student? The quarterback of the football team or something like that?"

"No, a man. He was my Driver's Ed teacher. I think he was also a gym teacher, but I'm not sure. I don't know why I liked him, looking back on it. He was sort of wiry and shifty-looking. But anyway he wasn't an old man like most of the teachers and he wasn't a greasy high school kid either, he was in between, in his mid-twenties, and I thought he was very attractive.

"We used to drive around in one of those cars that had two steering wheels and two sets of pedals. Usually it was packed with smelly pimply would-be-drivers, but after the first few times it always worked out that it was just the two of us. I was so nervous I can't tell you, partly because I had this crush on him but also because I couldn't drive to save my life, but he was very nice, made jokes, that sort of thing. I wasn't a very good driver to begin with and this situation made me almost inept. So he did most of the driving from the passenger's seat while he talked to me, and I just clutched my wheel as he steered his, which was in some ways a very sexy experience, having the wheel move in my hands like that."

"This is your big confession?" Michael was in fact extremely excited to hear this but wanted to play it down. He assumed there was more to come.

"Not exactly," she said. "On what was supposed to be my last lesson he put his hands between my legs. I was totally freaked out and didn't say anything. He undid the button on my jeans and got his hand in there and we didn't say a thing, we just kept on driving. Then he unzipped his pants and he took us on the highway and he put my hand on it and said, 'Now you are going to learn how to drive with one hand.' And I gave him a hand job as best as I could while we sped down the highway and he fondled me. I learned more from that guy about hand jobs than I did about driving. I failed my driver's test after that and didn't take it again until I was in college."

"Did he come?" asked Michael, trying to sound as clinical and disinterested as possible.

"All over the dashboard. I was shocked. We nearly crashed." She paused for a moment. "I didn't, though."

"Did you ever see him after that?"

"I saw him around but we never spoke after that. He would smile at me. I was totally grossed out. It was the first one I ever touched."

"That's not a very romantic introduction to penises," he said.

"I can't imagine a romantic introduction to penises," she said. "Now you tell me something."

"Yours wasn't so bad."

"Go ahead," she said.

"Well," he said, and there was a pause, during which Jane tried to imagine what he would say. She suspected he would admit to having made out with another guy in college or having done heroin for a period of a few weeks. Part of her was hoping for something extremely outlandish, and part of her was hoping for some small innocuous scandal.

"I went to a prostitute once," he said.

This surprised her a little but it didn't shock her. She mentally filed it under the heading of small scandal. She shifted her body against him, mingling her feet with his.

"Tell me what happened," she said.

"Does that shock you? Do you think it's horrible?"

"No," she said. It was the truth.

"I had a car at the time. It was a few years ago. It was one of those huge old American cars from the mid-seventies that growl. An Oldsmobile. It was tan. Sort of the color of frog throw-up. It had a dent in the back."

"Tell me what happened on the inside of the car."

"I was drunk, I think. It was late, I was drunk, it was summertime. I was driving somewhere late at night and I came upon this row of prostitutes on the street. You know how they're sort of in rows sometimes, like, for a stretch of four blocks they'll be on every corner or something like that? Well, that's what this was, except it wasn't anywhere where you expect it. I forgot where it was, but it wasn't near Times Square or the meatpacking district. Park Avenue South, I think it was."

Jane was quite sure that if required he could go put his finger on the exact square foot of pavement his car had stopped on, but she let him have his vagueness.

"And I was completely surprised to see them, in a row like that," he went on. "And I circled back and drove by again, just looking. And I did this a couple of times, drive by like that . . ."

"So what happened with the prostitute? Get to the point."

"I'm getting there! God." There was a pause, during which Jane resolved to be patient. In spite of her assessment of this as only a small scandal there was something about his jittery voice as he told the story that was making her ill.

Michael, for his part, was suddenly very unsure that what he was saying was in his own best interest. But he had started it, he thought. But, he reconsidered, he was still very far from finishing it. He tried to sense what Jane was feeling but couldn't tell exactly. Then, like an enzyme, his desire to confess kicked in, and he continued.

"Anyway," he finally said, "I drove past a few times at first thinking I would just look, but there was this one girl who was on the corner who looked pretty and somehow attractive to me. She was Puerto Rican, I think. After about the third time I went by, all of them were making these lewd gestures to try and get me to stop, but this one girl was just sort of hanging back from it all, standing there chewing gum like she was waiting for somebody to come by and give her a ride or something, except if you weren't a prostitute you wouldn't be waiting for somebody at four in the morning next to all these prostitutes.

"I stopped right in front of her. She walked up to the window like she had something much better to do but this would be all right for now. We talked for a minute and then she got in and told me what block to drive down and where I could park. I asked her if she used condoms and she said that she did, and I felt kind of relieved because somehow it made her seem safer, even though I had no idea what it would be like to get a blow job with a rubber on. . . ." He paused to check for any reaction in Jane, but whatever it was, she was concealing it. All the logs in the fireplace were burning full force now.

"So anyway, she was, like, pretty young and I . . . I can't quite explain it, she had this very fresh-faced and at the same time kind of sultry look, like she had had a lot of sex with her boyfriend in high school but had never really done this before. And then . . . this is the part that is deep and dark, I mean, I don't even know how you feel about the prostitute thing, you might, like, never talk to me again, but it doesn't seem that way. I would have just stopped after I said I went to a prostitute if you seemed totally appalled and freaked out and everything."

"I'm not freaked out," she said. "What did you do with her?" she said, as plainly as possible, making sure to suppress the curiosity in her voice.

"Well, I, uh, I wanted her to, like, act out this scene with me, in which she was this secretary at this big corporation that I was the president of or owned or something like that, and I was giving her a ride home for some reason, and then I pull over onto the side of some road and tell her that she's really nice and I like her but that she can't do her job for shit and that if she doesn't give me a blow job I'll have to fire her. I told her this and she looked at me a little skeptically, like, 'Oh, brother.' But then she said, 'All right. What's your name?' and I said, after a moment's thought, 'Mr. Peters,' and she looked at me even more, like, 'Yeah, right, give me a break.' And then I said, 'What's your name?' and she said, 'Ms. Valpecello,' and she was so casual about it that I thought it might actually be her real name. Then I started talking in this really low, sort of calm matter-of-fact slimy businessman voice about how nice she is and how nice it is to have her around the office. . . ." His voice trailed off.

"Was it nice?" she said.

"Yes. I don't think 'nice' is the word I would use, but it was what I wanted. It was more than what I wanted, actually."

"Was she good at it?"

"She was very good at it. She really got into her role. For a minute I thought she would rather quit her job than go through with it."

"I meant the other part. Was it good? Was she good at that?"

"It was all right," he said. There was something in the tone of Jane's voice that made Michael feel he should back off.

Jane didn't say anything. The only sounds in the room were the crack and hiss of the burning logs. The room was quite warm now, and completely still, except for the swaying flames in the fire and the faint rise and fall of their chests as they breathed. Jane felt a tightness in the soft spot between her ribs. His interest in her being Hispanic and his apparent relish in her youth was disgusting and pathetic, she thought. And yet even as her insides tightened as though they had just received a dose of awful-tasting medicine, something else was expanding inside of her, opening toward Michael. She wouldn't have expected something like this from him, and in an odd way she liked that he had done something so extremely sleazy and then told her about it. If life were lived under optimum conditions, she wondered, would there be more of this kind of self-exposure, or less? Were secrets between lovers necessary? Were they possible? Or was it only a matter of time before they all came spilling out? And then what happens, when all the secrets are used up?

The scale of her disgust and attraction hovered, each side weighted down evenly, and the result was silence.

"What are you thinking?" he said after a little while.

"I'm not sure," she said.

"Are you horrified?"

"I'm tired. This day has been exhausting."

Those were the last words of the night. Jane rolled over and curled up away from Michael, the ridge of her spine emerging from her back like a guardrail.

Michael lay on his back, wide awake, wondering if he had just squandered his relationship with Jane, and thinking about Ms. Valpecello. When they were done she had slid a long manicured fingernail the color of a fire engine underneath the edge of the rubber, sliding it off deftly and putting it in a piece of tissue she had ready for the occasion. The movement had all the soothing assertiveness of a nurse tending to a slightly injured patient, and for a moment Michael was suffused with the kind of overwhelming gratitude someone might feel for a doctor or a mother. Just then, at the height of his feelings for Ms. Valpecello, a police car rolled by slowly, two police officers with mustaches drifting into view as if they were going by in a gondola.

"Don't worry," said Ms. Valpecello, who was still, he noticed much to his amazement, chewing a piece of gum. "We could pretend we're boyfriend and girlfriend." She said it so sweetly and matter-of-factly that Michael had no trouble imagining it at all. He was desperately sad when she got out of the car.

He looked at Jane's back and tried to imagine, from the pace of her breathing, what she was thinking. He hoped that perhaps some court scene had raged in her head and that he had emerged Not Guilty.

After a few minutes he realized she was asleep. It surprised him but then he remembered that she had drunk a lot of wine. Perhaps the court scene was continuing anyway. He climbed out of the bed and looked down at her, wondering what she was dreaming.

He took the bottle of brandy and a snifter off the mantel and lay down in front of the fire, which he fortified with another log. He poured himself a generous portion and drank the whole glass staring at the fire and looking at the black hole into which the smoke flew up, his eyes watering slightly every time he brought the glass to his lips.

Jane woke up to the sound of someone groaning. Her mouth was incredibly dry and her head felt as if it weighed more than the rest of her body. She sat up and surveyed the room. It was dark and hot; there were still embers in the fireplace. She stared at them vacantly for a minute, thinking they looked like a crocodile. Eventually something broke and the embers shifted and the crocodile no longer had its jaw and didn't look like a crocodile anymore. It looked like Noah's Ark. She heard the sound again, someone coughing. It came from the bathroom, which she noticed for the first time had the light on. The toilet flushed.

She walked to the door and opened it. The bright white light leapt at her and she covered her eyes. When she opened them she saw Michael kneeling in front of the porcelain toilet bowl. He seemed to have just finished throwing up. He turned his head to look at her. His face was extremely flushed and his lips were wet and a little swollen-looking. His hair was tousled.

"I drank all the brandy and fell asleep in front of the fire," he said in explanation.

He got to his feet, put the lid down on the toilet, and sat down, ankles splayed apart but knees brought protectively together. He looked up at her standing in the doorway, a little befuddled. They were both naked.

They looked at each other for some time. Michael stared at the smooth soft curve of Jane's stomach and then at her breasts and their pale round nipples. He felt in awe of her, of how beautiful she was. Then he looked at her face, and her eyes. They held each other's gaze until he broke the silence and said, "Do you feel differently about me after what I told you?"

"Yes," she said.

"For the worse?"

"Maybe," she said again.

"It doesn't have any redeeming qualities?"

She didn't answer, just looked at him on the toilet for a minute, enjoying his uncertainty. Then she walked over to the sink, unwrapped one of the glasses that sat on the counter, and filled it with cold water.

She drank it down in several gulps and then filled it again. "Drink this," she said. He took a few tentative sips and then gulped the rest. She took the glass from him, filled it again, and then drank from it until it was empty.

"Are you all right?" she said.

"Yeah," he said. "I'm fine."

She stepped out of the bathroom. In a moment she came back with a small shiny object in her palm. She started unwrapping it.

"It's the after-dinner mint they left on the night table."

She carefully snapped it in the middle and handed him half. They looked at each other as the minty taste spread around in their mouths. The taste was delicious. They chewed and began to grin dumbly at each other. Just then, they were both incredibly happy.

THE DARK PIANO

"ALEXANDER!" his mother called from the kitchen. "Alexander?"

It was so familiar, these two inflections, like opposite halves of a broken cookie—the first a statement, the second a question, as if perhaps he had fallen out the window sometime in the last half hour.

"What!" he yelled back from his room. He was waging a war of attrition against his mother, one sullen moment at a time, and was not in an agreeable mood—she had provoked him with the simple comment "No more TV until your grades improve." His strategy was to go into a low-level sulk that would not be obvious at any given moment but would have a cumulative effect, like radiation.

"I need to talk to you," came the voice from the kitchen. "Come here!"

He went grudgingly into the kitchen, careful not to betray any emotion when he saw her. Without thinking he walked past the table where she sat, opened the refrigerator, and stared into it for nearly a minute, as if a delicious and unexpected treat would materialize if he stared long enough.

When it didn't, he gave the refrigerator door a slight tap and went and sat across from his mother. The small square table had a chair on each side. The one to his left was stacked with old newspapers. The one to his right was empty. It used to be his mother's seat, but now she was sitting across from him, in the chair that used to be occupied by his father.

"Well," said his mother. She was trying to be amicable. He stared at the table sullenly. The ban on television had been in effect for a week. It was a drastic action on his mother's part. His teachers had told Alex he was an underachiever. He thought it had a nice ring to it. Apparently they had told his mother something much worse.

"So," she said. They sat in silence for a moment. Alex could tell she was noticing his subtle campaign of unfriendliness. Something inside of him rebelled against the idea of intentionally making his mother unhappy, and he considered cracking a slight smile. But then he remembered his goal of having television reinstated, which took priority over everything, and he made his face even more glum.

"I can see you are not in the most splendid mood right now," said his mother. She paused at this, her eyes smiling, and then without any warning Alex burst into a laugh, more like a tight-lipped giggle, which he then violently repressed.

"Well all right," said his mother. "I'll just look at your forehead while we talk. It's a nice forehead."

Alex shook his head so that his hair fell over his forehead. His hair had grown so long that he could actually chew on it when seized by the impulse. When one of his teachers confronted him after class about yet another failed test, he had explained that chemicals from his shampoo had caused brain damage but that it wasn't all bad, because they were going to sue the shampoo company and spend the rest of their lives living off the profits.

"Oh God," said his mother now, laughing and looking at the ceiling. "Well, what I wanted to tell you is that I've taken a new job." She was serious now. "I'll be working for the Metropolitan Museum of Art, as a fund-raiser."

Alex felt a shiver of anticipation run down his back. Her tone of voice suggested that this news meant that somehow there would be a change in the natural order—as dictated by her—of their lives, and since he was so miserable just then, any change held out the possibility of improvement.

"This is a necessity," she continued, "but you don't need to think about that. All you need to think about is pulling yourself together at school. It's a very good school and you don't want to have to leave it."

Actually Alex would have liked nothing better than to leave it, but there was no point in saying that.

"The good news is that we are going to be all right," his mother went on, straining for optimism. "I mean we're always going to be all right. I don't want you to worry about that. But our schedule is going to change. My job is in the evening. So when you come home from school, I won't be here."

Alex could already feel the smooth bedcover of his mother's bed pressed against his cheek as he lay sideways facing the television.

"The change," his mother continued, "will be that you will be on your own in the house while I am gone, and you will have to behave responsibly. I'll leave some dinner for you to heat up, and you will have to go to bed by yourself. The change will *not* be"—she accentuated the "not"—"that you will start watching television."

Alex looked up at his mother with the most innocent and unassuming expression he could muster, but he could tell from the way she was looking at him that he hadn't been able to suppress the delighted gleam in his eyes.

"Come here," said Alex to the girl walking down the hall. It was a long hall with windows and a white tiled floor, and just then it was dead silent in a way unique to junior high schools when class is in session. Alex was sitting in front of the door where his seventh-grade English class was taking place. Earlier that day he had discovered a new function on his Timex watch—when held at the proper angle it reflected a small dot of light. He had spent the first half of class studiously keeping the dot on Mr. Astor's forehead until he screwed up and got it in his eyes and Mr. Astor made him sit outside.

"Come here, I wanna show you something," said Alex again. The girl, who was in fifth grade, regarded him with the suspicious eyes of a nervous animal. She was wearing a red down jacket. Strands of sandy blond hair were already escaping from her ponytail and it wasn't even lunch yet. Her knees, which were extremely knobby and covered in blue stockings, slowed to a halt in front of him.

"I wanna show you something," said Alex again. "It's a test. An intelligence test. You're intelligent, right?"

The girl kept her lips tightly pursed and nodded only slightly.

"Well then, look." He took out three playing cards, two black and one red, flashed them at her, and then began to toss them back and forth on the hallway floor. "Red you win, black you lose. All you have to do is pick the red card, and you're smart."

He tossed the cards very slowly and asked her to point to the red card. She did, and he turned it over.

"You got it! Wow, you must be really smart," he said. "Try again."

He had been spending a lot of time watching the three-card monte players who lined up on Broadway between Forty-fourth and Forty-fifth Street, listening to the rhyming phrases they repeated over and over and trying to learn their tricks. He was well acquainted with the system of lookouts and shills and hustlers; it was like a conspiracy against the established order of things that he was in some way a part of, if only in spirit. He could see a potential mark halfway down the block, and it gave him a strange thrill to watch unsuspecting tourists lose their money. It was sickeningly funny and sad to watch them pull large bills out of the unlikely places they had been stashed for safety—out of socks, from under hats, out of a tiny pocket sewn into a pants cuff—only to then hand the money over to a man huddled over a flimsy stack of cardboard boxes, while his assistants cooed with fake consolation and tried to get another bet out of them.

There was always that intense moment of incredulity as they reached for the card they were sure was red, flipped it, and then froze in disbelief when it turned out to be black—a ten of clubs or an ace of spades. He would watch their necks redden and try to overhear their pathetic explanations to whomever they were with: "I'm sorry . . . I was sure . . . I can't believe it!" He pitied them, and yet he would follow them down the street after they had slapped down as much as a hundred dollars on a sure thing that turned out to be wrong, just to observe the body language of humiliation. What had been sacrificed in this gamble? An evening at the theater, a day at the ballpark, that special last-night-in-New York dinner? Every step and gesture screamed with defeat and anger and embarrassment; it was a spectacle that hypnotized him.

"Listen," Alex now said to the girl after he had run the cards a few more times, letting her win each time. "If you get it again I'll give you two dollars." He removed two crumpled dollar bills from his pocket and showed them to her, just like the guys on the street who waved thick wads of twenties and fifties in front of their victims' noses. The girl looked at the two dollars and then at Alex. She still hadn't said a word so far. Just nodded and pointed. "All right," she said now, her voice a little more spiteful and confident than Alex expected. Probably a popular girl, he thought.

He flipped the cards faster this time and started in with the patter he had listened to so often. "You lose with black but the red gets twice your money back. . . . Red, red like a juju bean. . . . Black you lose, red you cruise. . . ." He flipped the cards, making his switch expertly, and sat back to wait for the girl's response. She reached for the card she thought was the red—but wasn't—and was about to turn it over.

"Wait!" he said at the last minute. "You've got to show me a dollar. How can I pay you if you don't have a dollar? You've gotta have your end covered too." She produced a dollar from a pocket in the huge red down jacket that she was wearing. Her whole physical presence was the puffy red jacket supported by the blue spindly legs and topped by the innocent wispy blond hair.

"All right," said Alex. The girl reached out and turned the card over, letting out a small pained gasp. Unfortunately Alex missed the expression on her face, which he had been so looking forward to, because at just that moment Mr. Astor had opened the door to let him back in. Instead of the girl's shocked face Alex saw Mr. Astor's bearded face, its stern expression exploding with outrage.

"Alex!" he shouted. "This is totally unacceptable behavior! Go to Ms. Farson's office right now. Right this second!"

"He made me do it!" yelled the girl, her voice squeaky, her dollar bill still clenched in her tiny fist.

Since he considered the return of television assured with his mother's departure from the house, he had broken his sulking campaign. His mother was predictably angry when the school called her to say that Alex had yet again been put on behavioral probation, to go along with the academic probation he had been on all semester. What was less predictable was the element of concern that darkened her expression; this was on the heels of a summer-long infatuation he had had with Off Track Betting. Alex had spent the better part of every day for two months hanging around the dingy insides of the OTB on Seventy-second Street and Broadway making friends with the other men and smoking fifteen-cent cigars as he carefully placed two-dollar bets on each race, consulting the *Daily Racing Form* for advice. It was a community, and he liked the white shoes, bulging stomachs, and yellow teeth of his fellow gamblers; it made him feel adult.

One day, while deeply involved in a debate about the Exacta in the seventh race with his friend Hectore—a man Alex liked enough to overlook the friendly pat on the crotch he occasionally administered—he noticed his mother standing right in front of him, her face a pale death mask of unhappiness.

The combination of her unhappiness and the sheer disturbing incongruity of his mother inside OTB was enough to get him to quit. But he was reminded now of that expression. It provoked a strange set of feelings that rumbled around somewhere deep within him, like the boiler of an apartment building emitting groans that are only barely audible to the building's residents.

The job started the following week. Alex had liked the sound of it, *Fund-raiser for the Metropolitan Museum of Art,* but he soon discovered that the exact nature of the job involved sitting in front of a telephone and calling people she didn't know to try to get them to give money over the phone. This wasn't what he had had in mind, and the more he thought about it, the more it alarmed him.

He was currently in the throes of a massive sleep-over phase, in which he would spend entire weekends at the apartments of his friends, all of whom were at least wealthy, if not filthy rich. Having a millionaire parent seemed to be a primary criterion for admission to his high school, and Alex frequently wondered with amazement how exactly the school had been able to confuse his mother with one.

One friend lived in the Dakota on Seventy-second Street and Central Park West. The entrance was always flanked with groupies waiting to catch a glimpse of the building's most famous resident—John Lennon. The doormen knew him, and he took great pride in the fact that they always let him in without calling upstairs. Walking past the gargoyle-festooned entrance, stained black with a century of soot, Alex felt the thrill of privilege; that he was just visiting was a mere technicality. It was a castle in which he was welcome. The idea that his mother might end up on the phone with his friend's parents asking for money made him faintly ill.

On the first day of his mother's job he raced home, looking forward to the six-o'clock news. He hadn't seen it in over a week and was starting to feel out of touch with the various murders, rapes, and accidental deaths that were constantly taking place around the city.

It was late November. When he stepped out of the elevator onto the landing and put the key in the front-door lock, it occurred to him that it would be dark in the apartment.

There had been a time when Alex was afraid of the dark, but that was in his childhood, a period which he considered to be a concluded episode in his life. Still, the darkness gave him pause. In the childhood he had left behind, Alex's strategy for coping with a dark house had been to whip himself into a frenzy and then charge through the house whooping and screaming while he turned on all the lights, making sounds that were a hybrid between the attacking Indians in old western movies and someone executing a karate chop.

Now he merely took a deep breath, marched to the lamp in the foyer, and turned it on. To his right was the kitchen, and to his left was the wide entrance to the living room, inside of which lurked, like a monster, a Steinway baby grand piano. The space underneath the piano was always the most frightening part of the darkened apartment, because it seemed like the most logical hiding place for a killer, a rapist, or a ghost, and in his earlier days his war whoops would reach a fever pitch as he approached it.

Now he walked towards it calmly, its faint outline visible in the light from the foyer. He had almost reached it when a convulsive animal instinct took over and he dropped into a fake combat stance screaming "Ha-yah! Ayyy-ya!" Then he was silent, and the apartment was silent with him, unmoved by his outburst. He stared, panting, into the dark space under the piano for several seconds. Then, as if he were approaching an enormous animal that he wasn't sure was dead, he scurried forward carefully and turned on the lamp that sat on top of it. Suddenly the piano became a piano and the space beneath it became a disheveled pile of boxes and crates filled with papers that, for some reason, his mother deemed too important to throw away. With this taken care of, the rest of the house came easily, and in no time he was lying with the television turned on, his dinner nicely laid out on a tray in front of him, and a little pastry waiting in the refrigerator.

This was the routine that developed over the course of the week. Every evening he would come home, having endured another excruciating day at school and two hours of detention after it, and, after engaging in a brief shouting match with the piano, plant himself comfortably in front of the television.

He would watch until the last possible moment, when he heard his mother's key insert itself into the front-door lock. For some reason, his mother always paused at this moment. It was a habit he had noticed a long time ago; the key would go in the lock and then a few seconds would go by before it turned. This small gap always puzzled Alex. He pictured his mother sighing and staring blankly at the front door, as if she needed to compose herself briefly before she could face what lay behind it.

Now, though, he rejoiced in these unaccounted-for seconds, because they gave him just enough time to jump up, turn off the television, smooth out the part of his mother's bed he had been lying on, and sprint out of her room into his, where he would jump into bed with his heart pounding and immediately pretend to be asleep. His room was right next door, not more than ten steps away, but he ran these ten steps as if they were the last ten steps of an Olympic gold medal sprint.

Several nights into this brand-new arrangement, his mother came and sat on his bed. Every night so far she had come into his room while he lay still facing the wall and trying to breathe as steadily as possible. She had only looked at him for a moment on those nights and then gone back out, but now she sat on his bed with a manner that seemed to suggest that he should turn around and face her. He lay very still. After a minute she said, "You're not asleep."

"Huh?" he said, rolling over and rubbing his eyes.

"You're not asleep. Stop pretending."

"What?" said Alex. He considered confessing right away but decided against it. "I'm asleep," he said.

"Don't lie to me." She stood up. "Come with me."

Alex followed her out of his room and into hers. She went over to the television and put her hand on it. "Put your hand here," she said.

Alex knew this was a dire situation, and in a last-ditch effort to salvage it, he gently placed his hand over hers and looked at her with the most innocent and trusting expression he could muster.

"Put your hand on the television," she said.

He moved his hand off hers and onto the smooth plastic surface of the television, which was quite warm to the touch.

"It's warm," she said gravely.

"You mean the room?"

"I'm very serious," she said. He could tell she was. It was disheartening. "You are forbidden to watch any television until your grades improve. And I do not want you to lie to me. Ever! Do you understand?"

"Yes," Alex mumbled.

"Do . . . you . . . understand!" she repeated loudly, this time punctuating each word with a brief pause. Her lips were pressed together and looked thin and cold. Her whole face was devoid of its usual warmth. This was an increasingly common posture she was assuming—the disciplinarian. Increasingly familiar, yet the transition between her normal self and her authoritarian self was never fluid. It always seemed like a mask to Alex, but it was a mask she was wearing more and more often.

The next day, after having negotiated the piano and turned on the other lights, he went into his mother's bedroom and discovered that the television was missing. The small green stool on which it normally rested sat where it always had, but there was nothing on top of it. It looked profoundly strange in this condition, like a stairway to nowhere.

Alex went into a brief panic, before settling down to an inch-by-inch search of the whole apartment. It wasn't long before he found it, sitting in his mother's bathtub with a towel draped over it; the towel seemed at once ridiculous and heartbreaking, as it suggested to Alex that his mother intended not just to make a symbolic gesture *but to actually hide the television so he wouldn't find it*. He pondered the absurdity of this for a moment and then hoisted the television out of its secret quarters and put it back on the stool.

From that point on everything was normal. He watched the news, waded through some game shows, and drifted through a series of pleasantly mind-numbing sitcoms. He ate his dinner, which was waiting for him on the tray, the television all the more pleasing for its new illicit status. The only catch was that now, instead of jumping up and running into his room, he would have to exercise some restraint and turn the television off on his own, so he would have time to put it back in the bathtub before his mother returned.

This new system worked well for the first few evenings, but one night, having put the television back in the bathtub, he found himself in the unusual situation of being in the apartment by himself and not watching television. He decided to explore. He walked into the kitchen and stared into the refrigerator for a while, even though he wasn't hungry. Then he went into the study. The study was an interesting place usually, if only because it was the room in which his mother conducted her personal and business affairs and as such it was constantly a mess, as if there had been a blizzard of small scraps of paper, and each snowflake of paper had to be carefully inspected for possible importance before it could be thrown out. On the desk sat a photograph of his father, looking away from the camera with a vaguely disapproving expression, as though he couldn't believe what a mess his former study had become.

After a half hour Alex's mother still wasn't home. He took this to be a wonderful gift. Then he had the idea that he could plug the television in while it was in the bathtub. He went in and did this, sitting next to the drain while he watched the eleven-o'clock news, the sound of the announcers' voices echoing off the hard white porcelain of the bathtub as they related that evening's disasters.

Then he started to think how he would never hear the key sliding into the lock from this corner of the apartment, and how awful it would be if his mother caught him red-handed crouched in her own bathtub.

What would she do? he wondered. None of his previous infractions had provoked anything more than a combination of stern language, severe facial expressions, and restrictions like "no television." He couldn't imagine what lay beyond this threshold of punishment. Whatever it was would be painfully unnatural for his mother to administer.

His father had spanked him once and he had cried; it was almost a fond memory.

It was now midnight. He opened the refrigerator and, for the fourth or fifth time that night, stared into its brightly lit shelves in search of something to eat. These constant revisits had a purpose. A bottle of olives with pimientos, which on the first visit would seem absolutely repulsive, might by the fifth or sixth visit be transformed into something interesting.

It was while staring one more time into the refrigerator that he was struck with the fact that his mother was dead. It was a simple fact, illuminated by the refrigerator light. He closed the refrigerator door and contemplated what life would be like without his mother.

He would be alone in the house. He could stay up late. He could watch all the television he wanted. He could stop going to school. He could eat anything he wanted. Then there was the inheritance. It wouldn't leave him rich, but it might last for a while if he sold all the paintings.

Alex began to take yet another stroll around the house, but this time he did so with an appraising eye, as if he were an heir who was looking over his newly acquired property, which, in a sense, he was. He thought of his mother on the phone to his friend's parents, fund-raising. A wave of humiliation washed over him. But then it went away. His mother was dead, so it wasn't an issue anymore.

His mother's death didn't faze him. He checked himself by repeating it over and over again as if it were fact.

"My mother is dead," he chanted in a low droning voice as he walked around the house. "My mother is dead, my mother is dead, my mother is dead." After a while he made it into a tune, singing the words to the melody of the Mighty Mouse theme: "My mo-oh-ther is deaaaaad!" It really wasn't so bad, he thought, and he silently congratulated himself on his mental toughness.

He arrived in the living room, the most sumptuous room in the house. He had never spent that much time in the living room; it was slightly, implicitly, off limits. He surveyed it, reading it left to right, until his eyes rested on the piano.

In spite of a brief and torturous experience with piano lessons, Alex didn't know how to play a note. He would sometimes sit at it and arbitrarily press the keys, listening to the sounds and repeating certain patterns. His mother, however, could play. Sometimes she would play classical music, which always bothered Alex, or folk songs from her childhood in Israel, which were even worse. She would play some song from her youth and sing along in a sad melancholy voice, her face always smiling in fond memory of the time the song made her think about. For some reason Alex had an allergic reaction to these songs and the sound of his mother's singing. She had a sweet clear voice that sometimes wavered slightly with emotion, and that slight quaver was the worst part. There was a kind of raw emotion to it that made him cringe.

Now, he stood contemplating the piano. He thought about

the prolonged periods of nonuse it had. How solemn it looked. In the light, it was pretty and elegant, its black surface as smooth as still water. The keys were slightly cream-colored from age. Then he thought of what it looked like in the dark. A monster. He would have to contend with that monster every day for the rest of his life. An eternity of tense, crouched approaches, sharp diaphragm-clenching yells, wide eyes.

It was then, when the picture of the dark piano formed in his mind, that he felt the first sob convulse somewhere deep within him, like a wave that was starting very far out at sea but already visible. It took a moment, but when it crashed it flooded everything.

His mouth opened into a large sideways eight and stayed there for a long period of silence, until a sob came out, wrenching his body. He sobbed continuously for a minute and then, almost as abruptly as it started, it stopped.

Feeling vaguely refreshed, he wiped his eyes and walked into the kitchen, where there was a clock. It was 12:30 A.M. He went and sat in his mother's chair, contemplating what to do next, and then he picked up the phone and called the police.

The voice that answered was cold, almost metallic, sexless. It asked where his emergency was. Somehow this wasn't the question he was expecting.

"I don't know," he said calmly, and then burst into another round of hysterical sobbing, somehow pronouncing the words "My . . . mother . . . is . . . dead," while his body convulsed uncontrollably.

"Calm down," said the voice on the phone. "Just calm down and we'll send a patrol car over. Where are you located?"

But Alex couldn't talk anymore, so he hung up. For some

reason, as soon as the phone was back in its receiver, he stopped crying. Crying was exhausting and he could only do it for limited periods of time. He wiped his eyes and his nose and thought how silly he had been to get so upset. For one thing, he could deal with his mother being dead. He already had asked himself if he could handle it and the answer had been yes. And for another, he didn't know for absolute sure if she was dead. He tried to follow her in his imagination. He tried to picture the room full of telephones where she worked. He pictured her at a movie, or at the gym she went to, or at her friend's house. Then, like a camera zooming out, he came to see New York in its entirety, sprawling endlessly in a sea of dirt, flickering lights, rumbling automobiles and streetlights swaying in the wind, red then green then briefly yellow. His mother could be anywhere, lying on a street or in a gutter or in a trunk of a car. If he went outside to look for her he wouldn't know where to begin. She might never be found. It could be a mystery that would never be solved. The police would be stumped. They would be overworked and frustrated. They would have newer cases to deal with, simpler cases that would make them feel good when they solved them. And besides, he had already hung up on them; what did they owe him?

He stood up and walked around the apartment once more, this time turning on every single lamp that was present and functioning. With the house sufficiently bright he went back and sat in his mother's chair to think.

He thought about the fact that his mother was certainly dead. Then he thought about how she most certainly wasn't. She couldn't be dead. She was his mother. And besides, how could both his parents die? Then he thought about how that as good as sealed it: it was his fate. He was to be systematically stripped of everything he possessed, starting with his most prized possessions and going down. He wondered in what order the other things would go, which toys would go first, when the apartment would go, the piano, the television. Then he wondered if the fact that his father died first meant he was more important.

Then his eyes fell on a small tattered brown book that lay next to the phone. His mother's phone book. He picked it up. A clue. He opened it to the first page. At the top, in faded pencil, was the name Irving Abelin, 595-3850. He looked at the clock. It was 12:45 A.M.. He picked up the phone and dialed the number. It rang several times. Alex was patient. The ringing soothed him. He felt that something was being done, action was being taken, and in a little while that action would lead to his mother and everything would be resolved. The phone rang several more times. Then someone picked up.

"Hello?" came the voice. It was a woman's voice full of the surprise and mystery that comes in the moment between when someone picks up the phone and someone else speaks.

"Hello," said Alex. "May I speak to Eve Fader?"

"I think you have the wrong number," said the woman. She sounded irritated.

"Then can I speak to Irving Abelin?"

There was a long pause and some rustling sounds, a low unintelligible murmur between two voices, one becoming slightly louder with the sound of denial. He heard a woman's voice say, "I think someone is looking for your girlfriend," followed by a man saying, "Don't be ridiculous."

"Hello?" came the man's voice, brusque and husky with sleep.

"Hello. I was wondering if you knew where Eve Fader is right now?" said Alex.

"Who is this?" said the man.

"It's Alex Fader, her son."

"Oh. I haven't seen Eve Fader in years," said the voice. Then off to the side, "It's some old friend of mine's son."

"Oh. I thought maybe you might know where she is. She hasn't come home yet. Your name was in her phone book. That's why I called."

"I'm very sorry, I can't help you." Irving Abelin's tone softened a little now. "I wish I could give you some advice, but like I said, I really haven't seen your mother in years."

They hung up. Alex sat still for a moment and then started leafing through the phone book. His initial idea was to systematically call every name in it, but the first call had exhausted him.

His mother was in a gutter somewhere, in a ditch, raped, dead. The tremor of a sob started to rumble deep within him, but then it gave way to something else. A simple idea. He would appeal to God.

He took a small table and chair out to the landing where the elevator came, and began doing homework as an act of penance. He was reforming forever. To get the maximum repenting points possible he started with the subject he most loathed—French. He took out a stack of index cards. On one side was a word in English, on the other its French counterpart. He stared uncomprehendingly at each word in French before turning it over and finding out what it meant. Soir–Evening; Sucre–Sugar; Garçon–Boy. This went on for a long time, interrupted occasionally by small bouts of crying. While he cried he prayed to God to bring his mother back. He engaged in a dialogue with God, an entity with whom, up to this point, he hadn't dealt with extensively.

He apologized for never having taken Him very seriously before. He promised he would always do his homework. He promised that he would listen in class. He promised that he would clean his room and put the laundry inside the hamper instead of just throwing it in a big pile on top of it. He promised to listen while his mother played the piano and sang. He promised to never watch television except when he was allowed to. He promised to never berate his mother for not knowing a thing about sports. And he promised that he would never, ever, make his mother worry about him the way he was worrying about her now.

She found him asleep, his head resting on the table in front of him. Index cards with French words were spread out beneath his head, a thin pillow. She had been out with friends and had hoped he would have gone to sleep on his own, but she knew immediately what he had been thinking. She put her hand on his head and stroked his hair tenderly, marveling at how quickly roles can be reversed and then reversed again. She didn't know about the promises he had made to God, and she couldn't know just then, as his head moved groggily awake and he let out a cry of joy, that they would all be broken.

THE HOT DOG WAR

I T ALL BEGAN AS a conflict between Gray's Papaya and Taco Rico, who had peacefully existed side by side for years, on the corner of Seventy-second street and Broadway. Gray's Papaya sold various tropical juices that were supposed to make you live longer, and hot dogs. Between the juices and the hot dogs, one's life expectancy would presumably come out even. Taco Rico sold tacos, and had a small hot dog trade on the side. At both establishments a hot dog cost a dollar.

Walter Weil, recently graduated from college and with a lot of free time on his hands, would occasionally stop by for a hot dog at Gray's Papaya, a few blocks from his house. Sometimes he would stop for a taco at Taco Rico. The choice between a taco and a hot dog didn't occupy him throughout the day. He didn't dwell on it. And certainly he didn't expect it to have any bearing on his love life.

The initial salvo was fired by Gray's, which occupied the sizable corner location. Taco Rico was wedged into a narrow space next door, up the block on Seventy-second street. Gray's posted a sign declaring a hot dog special: ninety cents each.

Taco Rico, for reason's involving pride or economics or both, retaliated. Outside their storefront, they posted a larger sign which read: "The Best Hot Dogs in New York—85¢ each!"

Tension built. What was once a casual if somewhat messy corner populated by two stores and a newsstand turned into a riveting scene of people standing in front of the two establishments, deliberating about which place to buy a hot dog.

Walter was one of those people. His instinct was to be loyal, but since he had patronized both places in friendlier times, there was no one to be loyal to. When Gray's dropped their price to eighty cents, he bought from them. When Taco Rico came back with a price of seventy-five cents, he bought from them. It was a war of attrition, one nickel at a time.

He met Delia at seventy cents, standing in front of Gray's Papaya.

"You're supporting the competition," she said one breezy afternoon, without any effort to be friendly.

She had a slender neck and a wide pale face with long-lashed dark eyes. Her hair was short and brown and was topped by a peculiar pillbox hat that might once have been the favorite of somebody's eccentric grandmother. The combination gave her the appearance of a strange and aggressive flower.

He had been staring, as he sometimes did. It wasn't a rude or lascivious stare; it was the blank, lost-in-thought variety. He wasn't used to having the recipients of his stares, which often included such inanimate objects as the sidewalk, talk back. The exact thing he had been staring at, while standing in front of the newsstand on the corner, was the mouth of a woman emerging from Taco Rico.

"What do you mean, the competition?" he said. He had just emerged from Gray's.

"Gray's is the favorite. I tend to support underdogs against the establishment," said Delia.

"They happen to be cheaper right now. I guess I'm being mercenary."

They were both holding hot dogs. She had emerged from Taco Rico with a drink in one hand and a hot dog with sauerkraut in the other. She was managing to eat the hot dog with incredible grace and tidiness, something Walter thought impossible and never seriously attempted. Neatness was a question of technique, and he didn't have it.

"You were staring," she said.

"I do that sometimes," he said. "I didn't mean to be intrusive."

She looked, he thought, like a silent-film star. She wore a jacket with a narrow waist that flared slightly at her hips and brown bell-bottom trousers whose cuffs reached all the way to the heel of her shoe; her eyelashes were long and laden with mascara. Each blink took place as if in slow motion. Her eyes had the clear, impassive quality of someone who wasn't easily amused, but wasn't entirely beyond it either.

"You have beautiful eyes," said Walter. To say such a thing to a woman, let alone to one he had never met before, was so out of character that as soon as the words had left his mouth he felt a spasm of panic.

"Just look at the eyes of the Taco Rico man. They're getting darker by the day," she said.

She made a rather delicate maneuver, balancing the hot dog on top of the Styrofoam cup of Coke and reaching down to pick up a newspaper and stick it under her arm.

At the last moment she had to reach over and steady the hot dog. It was then that Walter offered to hold the Coke, and she let him. It was, he often thought in retrospect, their first moment of intimacy, since one doesn't let an absolute stranger hold one's Coke. Walter was so pleased with the situation he almost didn't want to give the Coke back after she completed her transaction.

But he did and she said goodbye, walking east on Seventy-second Street. As she walked away, Walter stared at her jawline. It was moving in a very attractive manner, and even after he stopped looking at it, he could picture it clearly.

He turned toward the newsstand, which was crammed with magazines dangling like Christmas decorations. There was a face on the cover of each one, looking at him. He looked at the faces and noticed one in particular; it moved. It was the Indian newsdealer's face, in his little box, peering out at him with a quizzical expression.

Women were like campfires to Walter: warm and comforting in the midst of the wilderness, but if you didn't keep an eye on them you might end up engulfed in flames. He generally played the role of cynic when his friends confided details of their own women-related problems. His own relationships tended to be groping and short-lived. He had had his fair share of sexual experiences, but he had come to think of sex as a form of roulette; once something was set in motion it was nearly impossible to control. Even these encounters had trailed off in the months since he graduated from college, and in their absence he was almost able to forget the completely nauseating terror of having a crush.

"I met a girl," Walter told his friend Augie. Augie was a little on the short side and his red hair had been prematurely thinning since college, but he was extremely energetic and vehement and had always done well with women. In fact, he talked about them incessantly, and Walter assumed he would be interested in talking about his new acquaintance.

"I actually met a girl who I like," repeated Walter. He waited for Augie's congratulations.

"Bad news," said Augie. "Women are bad news if you don't know how to handle it, and you definitely don't know how to handle it. You're going to want things from them they're not going to be able to give. Then you'll stop wanting them. They're going to make you complacent."

"But I've been complacent long enough without any help from women!" said Walter. "Maybe I'm strange, maybe I have an inverted psychological metabolism, but I get very excited and active around women."

"That's just the point. All that excitement drains you of the energy you could be using to look inward and find something out about yourself. With women around you get excited about all the wrong things."

"Well, what are the right things?"

"It's not for me to say. But you have to be creative. Right now, I'm very excited about dissuading you from going out with this girl."

"We're talking about a few chance encounters here. I chatted with her in front of a newsstand and held her Coke. I'm not on the threshold of marriage."

"You're on the threshold of obsession," said Augie.

Walter began loitering in front of the newsstand in the hopes of seeing Delia again. He had been buying from Taco Rico exclusively, in spite of the fact that Gray's was a nickel cheaper just then, a mere sixty cents. So he was shocked to see her emerge from Gray's with a hot dog and what appeared to be a papaya drink.

"I'm confused by your behavior," he announced.

For a moment she appeared to be considering walking away, thwarted from her paper by a strange man, but then she recognized him.

"Oh, hi," she said. "What are you confused about?" She looked over his shoulder at the array of magazines behind him. "The magazines? I could suggest one. There's a wide variety of dirty ones which are all displayed prominently and then there are the respectable ones stacked neatly in the corner."

"No, I mean, you've just come out of Gray's after that lecture about the underdog and me being a mercenary."

"Oh. It's true," she said, suddenly pensive. "That's a little hypocritical, isn't it? It was the lure of the papaya juice, I think."

"Immortality is tough to resist."

She didn't answer, because she was chewing in that neat manner Walter liked so much. He introduced himself.

"My name is Delia," she said. Since her hands were full, they didn't shake.

"That's a nice name," Walter said, and immediately flinched internally at how banal he sounded.

"I don't know what came over my mother. Now she calls me Dee."

"Okay, I'll call you Dee."

"No, don't do that. Only my mother calls me that."

"I see," said Walter. "I wouldn't want to intrude on your mother's territory."

"No," said Delia, following the word with a blink as slow as a curtain call. "You wouldn't."

Suddenly the subway station across the street released a trainload of people who poured forth from the ancient brick structure with the enthusiasm of escaped convicts. The corner surged with activity.

"It was nice seeing you again," said Delia. Then she gave him a playful wink, one eye flicking shut and open in a solo performance. "You must really like hot dogs."

As she said this she was already turning away and joining the stream of people moving up the block, so the last word came nearly over her shoulder, accompanied by what Walter thought was a warm smile. After she had left he turned back to the newsstand, and his audience of one. Walter shrugged at the small man, who looked back inscrutably. It was just then that Walter realized he had forgotten to talk about his planned topic of conversation, which was that yes, the eyes of the Taco Rico man were getting very dark indeed.

When Walter was growing up everything he did seemed in preparation for something else. At his ninth birthday party someone asked him what he wanted to be when he grew up and he said, "Ten." He still considered it one of his wittiest moments. When he was in high school he had looked forward to college and when he was in college he always had one eye on the Real World, which was how he and his friends phrased it then, as if it were a glimmering city just over the horizon to be visited during summer vacation. After such a long buildup, however, the Real World was turning out to be a disappointment. It unnerved him to think that this was it, his life, in progress. The trailers were over, the movie had begun, but it had none of the benefits of a movie; you couldn't rent it later, you couldn't see it more than once, and you couldn't know ahead of time how long it lasted. There was the sneaking suspicion that somewhere along the line, he had missed an essential detail of how to live.

"Sometimes I wonder if some huge monstrous event is going to fall on me from the sky, something I'd never expect," Walter once said to Augie.

"You have to court calamity," Augie had told him. "You can't just wait for it to come to you."

Walter began to spend his late afternoons on the corner of Seventy-second Street, waiting for Delia to show up. It was a corner designed for passing through, not for hanging around, and Walter began to feel a kind of camaraderie with the corner's permanent inhabitants—the newsman, the man at the takeout window of Gray's, the Taco Rico man. It was early spring, and the whole city was experiencing the slight lift in mood that comes from the discovery that it is pleasant to be outside, and one needn't constantly rush to the next enclosed, heated space. People began to unfurl their bodies and stretch out; a sense of expansion was in the air.

It wasn't long before Delia came by again, part of a huge rush of people springing forth from the subway station. She didn't stop for a paper or a hot dog, so Walter had to jog to catch up to her. At the last moment he realized he had nothing to say and froze. But she had noticed him by then.

"You're staring again," she said. It was true. Walter was staring intently at the soft and, he thought, forgiving contour of her lips.

"I'm sorry," Walter said. "It's a bad habit."

"You seem to be on this corner a fair amount," she said. Every sensory mechanism in his entire body was flung forward trying to tell if she was being friendly or if she thought he was some potential weirdo who ought to be discouraged. His sensors couldn't provide any conclusive evidence one way or another. Just then Walter had the incongruous thought that he seemed most attracted to women who held out the possibility of disaster.

"I like hot dogs," he said.

"Another bad habit."

She blinked. Her head seemed to pivot slightly as if a thought pertaining to the man in front of her had just registered.

"Bye," she said.

She had taken several steps down the block when Walter lurched into action, running up beside her and blurting out an invitation to have a drink, to exchange phone numbers. As he said it, he nearly shut his eyes, as if he were going over the top of a roller coaster.

She paused for a moment, head pivoted, another thought. "All right," she said, eyes open, and in no time he had her number in his pocket. The whole thing happened very quickly.

"Something excellent has happened," exclaimed Walter.

"What?" said Augie attentively. Augie was always happy for his friend's good fortune, whenever some of it rolled around.

"Delia. I asked her on a date. I mean, I have her number, we talked about a date, we basically have a date."

"Who's Delia?"

"The girl! How could you forget about the hot dog girl?"

"Oh, from the newsstand. You have a date. Well, this is either the beginning of the end or the end of the beginning. I don't know which would be worse."

Walter paused a moment to wonder whether Delia had referred to him as "the hot dog man" in conversation with her friends. The thought made him sad and exhilarated. He imagined becoming part of her life, having overlapping friends, private jokes. Embracing on a crowded street as people rushed by.

"Augie?" said Walter in that tone of voice that people take on when about to ask for a favor. "I was thinking that perhaps you could join Delia and me for our first drink. It might take the pressure off, make it more casual, you know."

They were huddled in a dark crowded bar called the P&G on Seventy-fourth Street, hunched close over a small table in the back. Walter and Augie drank beer from bottles. Delia had a scotch with ice.

Walter realized after he had introduced Delia and Augie that he didn't know her any better than Augie did; they were more or less on equal ground as far as familiarity went, and the conversation proceeded accordingly, like three people meeting for the first time. It annoyed Walter, because he had invested a lot of energy in contemplating Delia, her body, her demeanor, imagining a history for her, thinking of her naked and next to him, blinking softly.

"So," said Augie. "What do you do?"

"I'm a film student," said Delia. "I have a day job, but that's what I really do."

Walter wanted to know what her day job was, because he had spent hours standing around wondering where she was just then and what she was doing, but Augie responded before he got it out.

"Are you going to go Hollywood and sell out right away or are you going to be experimental and have integrity?" said Augie.

"I know a lot of people who are experimental and don't have integrity," said Delia.

"And I suppose it's possible to go to Hollywood and not sell out," said Augie, though he didn't really look like he believed it.

"I know people who have integrity and don't experiment," Walter chimed in. Both Delia and Augie looked at him as if he had just made an extreme non sequitur.

"I actually don't care what you do," said Augie.

"That's friendly," said Delia.

"I don't say that to be rude, it's just that people get so caught up in the whole what-do-you-do thing. I'm trying to get away from it."

"And what do *you* do?" she said.

"I'm not telling."

"So you're unemployed," she said.

"Recently graduated from college," said Walter. "We're professional college graduates." Augie was glaring at Delia, and she sipped her scotch mirthfully.

"Delia, where are you from, anyway?" asked Walter, ignoring their moment of hostile commiseration. He enjoyed saying her name.

"The North Pole," said Delia, directing the answer to Augie.

"I see. The ice goddess," said Augie.

"And you're from some tropical paradise, I suppose?" said Delia. "Straddling the equator, perhaps? Grow your own tomatoes as a kid?"

"I'm from Cozad, Nebraska," said Augie. Walter knew that Augie had once been slightly ashamed of this fact but then realized its novelty had a kind of cachet.

"His town apparently has the best-selling postcard in Nebraska," said Walter.

"All right, fine," said Augie. "Bring that up. I'm not ashamed. It says, 'Cozad, the alfalfa capital of the world.' It has this ugly-looking tin alfalfa sprout harvester in the picture. I admit it. I'll probably live to be a hundred considering the amount of alfalfa I ate as a kid."

"We'll all be better off for it," Walter said, in vague attempt at sarcasm. He sensed something disconcerting happening at the table, and as if to confirm his suspicions, he saw Delia's expression soften as she stared at Augie.

"Wow," she said faintly. "My first boyfriend, the big love of my life, sent me that exact postcard when we just started going out. It was when everything was just starting and it was very intense and romantic. He drove across country without me, and the one time I heard from him was when that postcard came. On the back the only thing written was 'To my sprout.' "

There was a meaningful silence. Walter felt himself withdraw, becoming a spectator; it was a role he often assumed even when it was he himself that was the subject of his watching, an audience to his own life. Delia took a sip of her scotch.

Then Augie spoke. "You fell in love with a guy who called you 'sprout'?"

Had Walter been afraid of what had happened, what had happened might not have happened. But it hadn't occurred to him, and so he blithely went into the evening, only to watch Delia and Augie connect.

Walter had seen this before. Augie never seemed to get into relationships cautiously, like someone stepping into a hot bath. He got into them the way people step into unexpectedly deep puddles.

"I hope you don't mind," said Augie, genuinely concerned.

"Of course I don't mind," said Walter, minding terribly.

"If you guys had been involved I never would have let things happen, but I thought since it was just this passing thing, I mean a thing in passing."

"Yes, yes, Jesus," said Walter. "It's not a big deal. I knew her from the street."

Walter's relationship to Augie went through the subtle and unspoken transition friendships go through when one party becomes involved with someone. Walter insisted to himself that it was no big deal, and in a way it wasn't. His schedule didn't change. It wasn't as if he suddenly had more time on his hands. Augie was discreet enough not to talk about the romantic aspects of his time with Delia.

And Walter still spent time on the corner, though not as much. The taste of hot dogs had become inexorably linked to Delia, and thoughts of Delia were now accompanied by a tightening in his chest; the sight of a pack of eager, sprightly people springing forth from the exhausted-looking subway station made him retract a little and want to go somewhere more private, where there wasn't so much paper and debris swirling around his feet.

One fateful day, Gray's delivered what was clearly intended to be a knockout blow in the hot dog war. The entire outside of the store was painted white, with the words "Hot Dog Revolution! Fifty Cents!" scrawled urgently in thick black paint. It gave the store a kind of Berlin Wall feel. The new image worked. The store was packed with papaya-swigging, sauerkraut-chomping customers. Next door, Taco Rico had amended their sign to read: "The Best Hot Dogs in New York! 50¢!" But there was a decided absence of grandeur to it.

Feeling that the funereal mood of Taco Rico was much closer to his state of mind, Walter went in. The man's eyes were quite dark. The store was fairly quiet.

"What can I do for you?" said the man behind the counter.

Taco Rico closed sooner than Walter had expected, and a sign appeared, also sooner than Walter had expected, announcing the imminent arrival of an electronics store. And the electronics store opened sooner than Walter expected, so the whole corner was transformed quite quickly.

In the window of the electronics store, among all the other gadgets, was a video camera attached to a large color television. The camera was aimed right at the newsstand. Walter's routine changed slightly. Now when he bought a hot dog (for the low price of fifty cents, two dogs and a medium tropical drink for a dollar eighty-five!) he would wander over to the newsstand to eat it and browse, except sometimes instead of looking at the newsstand, he'd watch it on television, where he could also watch himself eating. There he would be, and behind him all the faces on the magazines, and behind them the little Indian man in his box who was also looking at the TV screen, which seemed to have him so transfixed he could barely be bothered to deal with his customers.

Once, Walter and the Indian man stared directly into each other's eyes, both pairs of which were trained on the screen. The two of them looked at each other, their gaze suspended. Without thinking, Walter smiled and waved. Much to his surprise, the Indian man waved back.

WORLD WITHOUT MOTHERS

WITH THE CAUTIOUS AIR OF a fugitive, Alex Fader arrived at the designated spot at the designated time and found himself alone. He was equipped with a bicycle, a wallet full of dollar bills, and several hundred reasons for why he was standing on Forty-eighth Street and Broadway at nine o'clock on a school night, in the event anyone asked. He locked his bike and then spent a few minutes trying to act natural, as if hanging out on Forty-eighth Street was something he did all the time. He forgot what it was that people do, exactly, when they act natural, so he resorted to unlocking his bicycle so he could lock it up again.

Nick arrived second. The two boys had been inseparably close friends once, but weren't anymore. Their years of friendship through junior high school had culminated the previous summer when they had both worked as bike messengers for the Educated & Dedicated messenger service. It made them close the way army buddies are close; they had experienced something the rest of the world couldn't really comprehend: oceans of pedestrians parting for them as they streaked kamikaze-style into intersections; ferocious battles with taxis, buses, and receptionists; the reassuring baritone of Tony, their dispatcher, who ended each and every sentence with the word "babe."

"Damn, it's weird to be here," said Nick, wrapping his heavy chain-link lock around Alex's bike as well as the adjoining signpost.

"Totally weird," said Alex. "What if we get seen?"

"What if we do? We're not doing anything wrong. We're just, you know, standing here."

They both stood silently for a moment as if to prove the point. Up the block a marquee blazed away shamelessly: THE OUI GIRLS.

It was a cool April evening, nearly half a year from the day Nick announced that they couldn't be friends anymore. The news came late one night after an evening of exploring the city on their bicycles, one of their great pastimes. They had climbed up on an enormous steamroller that was resting overnight, like an exhausted mastodon, in front of Nick's building on Eighty-eighth Street and Central Park West. Their bodies were splayed comfortably over the tangle of wires and levers when Nick broke the news. It was strangely like a breakup between a boy and a girl, though since neither of them had ever been involved in that, the comparison was not available at the time.

"Things just haven't been right with us," Nick had said. "I can't explain it. They just aren't going in the right direction. It's like we're holding each other back. We just can't hang out anymore."

Alex took this news badly but didn't show it. They sat in silence, an expanse of freshly rolled black tar stretched out beneath them, looking up at the black sky above. Alex periodically glanced over at the hugely pronounced bump in Nick's throat which bobbed wildly with each swallow. Eventually Nick went upstairs and Alex biked home, coasting west down the long slow incline of Eighty-sixth Street, the street lights a daisy chain of haloes stretching all the way to the Hudson River.

Nothing much changed after the steamroller conversation, and neither of them ever brought it up, but it lurked somewhere below the surface, informed certain situations, and now Alex reflected that standing here with Nick was different somehow than it might have been. It was like they were two actors at the start of a play, standing onstage and waiting for the curtain to rise; and everything before that moment didn't really count. It was practice.

A taxi honked and screeched to an abrupt halt, and Nick and Alex and everyone else on the block turned to look at it. A terrified face jolted into view in the backseat window. Then the taxi accelerated again and whisked the face away down Broadway, towards other near misses.

"They're not coming," Nick said.

"Are you sure?" said Alex. Besides the two of them, four others had committed to the excursion.

"John probably chickened out and Paul never does anything without John. Weinberg and O'Rourke are probably hiding under the covers pretending to be sick or something."

"Shouldn't we wait a little while longer, just in case?"

"I don't see why," Nick said.

They both turned to contemplate the bright marquee up the block.

Both Alex and Nick had slightly unusual family arrangements: Alex's father was dead, and Nick's was in Italy, which in some ways was worse. Save for a card at Christmas and occasionally on a birthday, he didn't keep in touch. Nick's mother, Helen, didn't pay much attention to him, and when she did, it tended to be sharp and intense attention, as often a reprimand as anything else.

Nick lived in an enormous apartment on Central Park West that belonged to his stepfather. The apartment was a maze of rooms, most of which were connected by a long hallway that was always dark. At one end of this hallway, tucked away at the back of the house, was Nick's room, a kind of fugitive outpost. At the opposite end was the master bedroom.

The stepfather's name was Harold, which Nick had amended to Harry as a subtle form of rebellion. Harry was a psychiatrist; he never spoke much and spent most of his time enclosed in either his room or his study, from which he would occasionally emerge smoking a cigar. He tended to move around the house silently, like a ghost, appearing in the kitchen or the hall suddenly and then wordlessly moving away. These appearances were like small moments of stopped time, as if the air had become electrified and any sudden movement would give its author an electric shock.

When Harry's children lived there the apartment had been full of sounds, but they were all adults now and lived elsewhere. Nick had two brothers of his own, but they had been sent to boarding school. So the apartment, with all its rooms and pockets of light and darkness, was occupied by three people composing two separate campsites at opposite ends of the long silent hallway.

Nick carried himself with the disposition of a war veteran who has seen sights so gruesome and horrific that everyday occurrences were doomed to banality by comparison. His body was very advanced for a fourteen-year-old, a mixed blessing, since along with his muscles, the hair in assorted and—to his classmates—surprising parts of his body, and the painfully conspicuous bulge in his swimming trunks came a violent attack of acne. Nick considered the acne to be part of a terrible conspiracy of fate against him. The combination of the muscles, the anger, and the sense that he was up against something unfathomably large and complicated gave Nick a vaguely messianic authority.

Alex himself was fat, or at least he was under that impression. He would occasionally get into enormous arguments with his mother in which she maintained that he wasn't fat, he was just a little heavy, and in fact quite handsome. Alex perceived this to be a prime example of his mother's refusal to accept reality even when it stared her right in the face—Alex himself was a complete fantasist, dreamer, and master of evasion, except in the presence of his mother, when he became a realist, a pragmatist, and an advocate of the cold hard truth.

In retaliation against his mother's unreasonableness, he would recite a litany of abuse which he routinely received from his classmates, usually ending with what he considered to be the most humiliating—Sperm Whale. The very existence of such a ridiculously titled animal seemed part of his fate. He delivered these lists in the cadences of a religious leader scolding his congregation for their sins, as if once his mother was presented with such irrefutable evidence ("How could the entire school be wrong about my being fat!"), she would have to acknowledge the truth. When he had finally exhausted himself of these details her response would be to look at him softly and say, "Well, I still think you're handsome no matter what."

Nick had no trouble acknowledging Alex's fatness, though

he wasn't mean about it. As a remedy he advised Alex to take two steps at a time whenever he encountered stairs.

Now, standing on Broadway with the traffic whizzing by, Alex reflected on the way things used to be between him and Nick. They were a good team—Alex, the talkative smart aleck, and Nick, the strong and sullen one, attractive to nearly everyone, it seemed, but too wound up to be approachable, even by extroverted, crush-stricken girls. That Alex was the exception to this rule gave him pride. They sat together at lunch, they got into trouble together at school with some frequency, and they moved through the city on their bikes, exempted from the laws of gravity everyone else had to abide by. But perhaps their biggest shared enterprise had been the eclairs, which might also have been their demise.

One particularly lazy Sunday the previous summer, precariously close to the advent of a new school year and the start of high school, they were lounging around Nick's room, broke and bored. Nick, who had a flair for cooking, suggested they make some eclairs, and Alex immediately amended that to making a lot of eclairs and selling them in Central Park. The division of labor would be that Nick would make them, with Alex as a kind of chef's assistant, and then they would go to the park with a big tray and Alex would be in charge of selling them, or, as Alex put it when they were flush with excitement about the project, "I'll do the marketing."

The first step in the process was to make the eclairs, which involved a major encampment in Nick's kitchen, an act that immediately lent the enterprise an element of danger, as any activity outside of Nick's room had the vague aura of a reconnaissance mission behind enemy lines. It was a Sunday afternoon and Helen and Harry were out of the house, the time of their return unknown.

Nick went about assembling all the necessary ingredients and utensils on the large kitchen table, explaining the function and purpose of each one to Alex as he went along. He took out flour, butter, sugar, a small bottle of vanilla, and some cooking chocolate. "This is terrible," Alex said after sampling the chocolate.

"It tastes better when it's cooked," said Nick. "That's why it's called cooking chocolate."

When all of this was laid out on the table they stood back and looked at it admiringly.

"All of this is going to turn into eclairs," said Alex. Then they began cooking. Nick was unusually animated, carefully adjusting the dials of the oven, pouring things into bowls, and instructing Alex on such details as to how to stir egg whites and how to squeeze cream through the icing dispenser, which was like a paper sock with a small hole at the toe.

They started around noon and by late afternoon they had entered Central Park, walking triumphantly with a tray of twenty-four homemade chocolate-covered cream-filled eclairs of generous proportions. They talked excitedly about where they should set down the small folding table which Nick had removed from one of the less-used rooms of the apartment, having decided on it after a long deliberation over which table was most portable, least valuable, and in general held out the least risk of complicating factors.

These complicating factors had been a faintly acknowledged backdrop to the entire cooking process; the entire time they were on guard for the sound of the key turning in the door. They only relaxed when they had cleared the front door of Nick's lobby because, as Alex put it, "We're in the public domain." And they had twenty-four eclairs—which with any luck they would turn into twenty-four dollars.

They settled on a location near the Great Lawn, an enormous dusty field with hardly any lawn encircled by a cracked asphalt road. They set up their table, and Alex began to make a few tentative attempts at soliciting passersby. Somehow the eclairs didn't seem as grand outdoors as they had in Nick's kitchen. At first no one stopped; only a few people looked at the two of them, standing gamely behind their little table.

Nick stared down as if in a trance at the array of eclairs neatly arranged in rows and then said, "They look like turds."

"They do not!" said Alex defensively, aware somehow that he was about to be abandoned.

"This is your part of the deal," said Nick, and then he went and climbed a tree a few yards away.

For a few minutes things looked bleak. Then someone stopped in front of the table. It was a young man with his face made up like a clown, minus the red nose. A polka-dotted jumpsuit protruded from the his shoulder bag. "Hi there!" said the clown. "I see you have eclairs here."

"Wanna buy one?" said Alex. "One dollar each."

"One dollar for an eclair! My God! What is this, the Oak Room at the Plaza Hotel?"

"These aren't normal eclairs," said Alex. "They're gourmet eclairs. Homemade."

"Gourmet eclairs!" said the clown. His enthusiasm seemed

very natural, he being a clown.

"That's right," said Alex. "That's the chef." He pointed up towards the branch where Nick was sitting.

"A chef in a tree!"

"Hello, Mr. Clown," said Nick, waving.

The clown bought an eclair, walked away, then came back and bought another one because, he said, they were delicious. "I just did a birthday," he said as he handed over his second dollar.

Bolstered by the clown's enthusiasm, Alex began to hawk the eclairs aggressively. People looked at him as they walked by. A man stopped and asked Alex if he could prove the eclairs hadn't been poisoned. He eventually left without buying one, unconvinced. A happy-looking couple in shorts stopped and bought two. Nick sat in the tree, stripping bark one tiny piece at a time. Whenever Alex made a sale he would point up to the tree and say, "That's our chef, the finest eclair chef in the world!" and Nick would wave halfheartedly at the perplexed-looking customers.

Central Park was bathed in the rich warmth that it sometimes acquires at the end of a nice day in late summer, when the leaves are at their most lush ripe green. The presence of two eclair-hawking kids, one chattering nonstop and the other up in a tree, seemed to appeal to people's expansive, upbeat mood. They sold out in an hour and a half, and walked back to Nick's house in a state of exuberance. The tray which Alex had carried into the park with such care and caution (Nick kept telling him not to drop it) was now dangling freely like a bike wheel at his side. They talked about how they would do this every weekend, maybe expand volume, hire their other friends as vendors. Each had twelve dollar bills stuffed into his pocket.

Helen took a dimmer view of the operation. When they got back to the apartment she yelled at Nick while Alex watched.

"You've shown complete disrespect for this kitchen and for me. Look at this." She waved at the state of the kitchen, which, in their haste to get outside, they had not cleaned up. "And furthermore, you showed disrespect for Harry, by removing a piece of his furniture without asking." She turned to Alex and told him he had to go home.

"I don't want to go home," said Alex.

"He doesn't want to go home," Nick repeated immediately, as though Alex spoke a foreign language.

Helen gave Alex an exasperated look. "You have a perfectly nice home with a perfectly nice mother. I don't see why you two have to spend all your time here!"

It was agreed that Alex would go wait for Nick in his room down the long dark hall. When Nick walked in a few minutes later he said, "We're not allowed to make eclairs anymore. My mother says it's not fair that I do all the work and she provides all the ingredients and that we split it fifty-fifty. And she says she doesn't want us using the kitchen as a factory."

They sat in silence for a while, looking out Nick's one large window. The window looked west, and normally one could see the sunset, but an enormous building was being constructed between Nick's room and the sun. Nick referred to the building as "the Penis." While it was being built he would occasionally tell Alex, "The Penis got bigger today."

The building was as tall as it was going to get, but they hadn't completed the walls, so the sun streamed through its half-finished skeleton, and Nick's room was dappled in a grid of glowing bricks of sunlight and shadows that fell over the room like a net.

After a while Nick said, "I don't know why my mom is such a total and complete bitch."

They were both quiet for a little while and then Alex said, "She really is."

They were silent for a long time after that, and then Alex went home.

Now, standing on Forty-eighth Street and Broadway, recalling the eclairs and the Penis and the peculiar formality of the end of their being Best Friends, it occurred to Alex that maybe he shouldn't have agreed with Nick so readily when he called his mother a bitch.

"Let's go," said Nick, motioning up the block. He had on that stern grim expression he got when he felt he was meeting a challenge.

The two boys began to walk towards the theater.

"Wait!" Alex said at the last moment. He stopped short, suddenly convinced that a close friend of the family was at that very moment about to turn the corner.

"What's the matter?" said Nick, letting a tiny bit of derision creep into his voice.

"I'm just checking the place out," said Alex.

Nick gave him a skeptical look and started walking towards the theater again. Alex followed.

"Dammit!" he said as they approached the box office, disappointment ringing through his voice. "The movie started half an hour ago. I hate missing the beginnings of movies."

"I don't think it matters," said Nick. "They're not big on plot."

Nick stepped up to the thick glass window and asked for two tickets. The woman behind the glass stared down at them as if they were strangers who had just rung her doorbell in the middle of the night.

"How old are you?" she said loudly.

"Nineteen," said Nick.

"The hell you are!" bellowed the woman. "Get out of here and go home to your mothers!"

Her tone seemed to imply that she was on the verge of calling them herself. As she spoke, Alex became acutely aware of the bright orange light under the marquee. He stepped away from it quickly.

"Damn," he said when they arrived back at their bikes. "I can't believe they checked for ID." He glanced longingly at the marquee and then said to Nick, "Do you want to get a soda?"

"No," said Nick. "Let's go somewhere else."

"Somewhere else?"

"Yeah. It's not the only place in New York, you know. We'll try somewhere smaller, more out of the way."

They unlocked their bikes and began to coast down Broadway. They moved slowly, in unison, keeping close. Walking around, they were two distinct units, but when they biked together they were connected, like some strange sea creature, fluctuating, hydra-like, changing speeds together, making turns, the silence between them somehow louder than the surrounding noise on the street.

They coasted past an arcade, the word FASCINATION spelled out in bright blinking lights. At Forty-fifth Street they turned right and headed towards Eighth Avenue, where they turned right again, moving uptown slowly, coasting on new pavement that had bits of shimmering ground-up glass mixed into the black tar. Nick pulled in front of a dilapidated old store with Christmas lights blinking incongruously in the window. The lights encircled a faded illustration of a woman, below which was written: "Peeps, 25 cents."

They locked their bikes to a signpost in a tangle of chains and went inside.

The interior was brightly lit and smelled of cherry disinfectant. An older man who looked as if he had once been handsome motioned them to the counter. "Would you two gentleman like some quarters?" he said.

Alex and Nick stood still for a moment, briefly stunned by the bright lights and the fact that they weren't being asked to leave; then they produced several crumpled dollar bills and dropped them on the counter.

"Back in there," said the man in a friendly, matter-of-fact manner. He gestured towards a flimsy curtain that hung at the back of the room.

They went through the curtain without saying a word and found themselves at the end of a hallway made of doors. The light in the hallway was a dim gauzy blue, and above some of the doors was a small red light. Several other men moved up and down the hallway, self-enclosed entities, occupying a shared space but completely oblivious to one another.

Instinctively, Alex and Nick each moved to one side of the hall, separating, as if they understood that to be in this hallway one had to be alone. They each browsed the suggestive photographs positioned next to each door, and after a moment Nick disappeared. Alex opened one of the doors that didn't have a light on above it, not knowing what to expect on the other side.

He stepped into a small closetlike space, and the door closed behind him. In front of him was a small television screen with a slot above it, like a pay phone. The space was so small Alex almost felt cozy. Then he looked down at his feet and was reminded of a James Bond movie he had seen. In it a man was standing in what he thought was an elevator, but then the floor fell through and he was sucked down a long narrow tube which led into a pool filled with man-eating sharks.

He stared at the floor for a few moments, and when it didn't move he slid some quarters into the slot. The closet-size space went dark, and the small screen in front of him came to life. Images danced onto the screen, shifting and changing before Alex's vaguely comprehending eyes. He looked at the screen as one might watch the large plate-glass window at an aquarium through which a whale is visible. He understood it to be a whale, but not for a moment did it occur to him that he would ever be in the tank. This was part of another world, one that simultaneously existed and didn't exist.

He glanced again at the floor, and in this moment of respite from the screen's images he thought, quite suddenly and unexpectedly, of Nick. What was he doing at that moment? Why weren't they best friends anymore? And then, even more unexpectedly, Alex thought of his mother, a thought so intrusive and unwelcome that his head jerked back up to the screen, as if to banish it. There was a sound of a coin dropping, like when one's quarter is about to run out in a pay phone. He looked up just in time for the screen to shut off and the light to come on; in that last glimpse he saw something heavy and blunt writhe snakelike out of a man's fly, its tip finding its way into the glossy red enclosure of a woman's mouth. Like the flash from an unexpected snapshot, that last image burnt itself onto Alex's mind, and no amount of blinking could remove it.

Outside, he stood next to the chained bicycles. The scenery hadn't changed, though it was somehow different. He stood patiently on Eighth Avenue, waiting for Nick.

When he came out their eyes met and each searched the other for signs that they had perhaps not experienced the right thing or were not reacting to it normally. Their expressions were like those of two kids who had overdosed on candy bars.

"What did you think?" said Alex.

"It was weird," said Nick. It seemed like a sufficiently specific answer. They began unlocking their bikes.

"Would you do it again?" said Alex. "I mean, if you could do it over?"

"Would you?"

"I don't know. Maybe."

"I'd do it again. But at a different place. That place was strange."

It occurred to Alex that it was possible that what Nick had seen was something completely different, something much more horrible, or maybe more wonderful. He had no way of knowing. He certainly wasn't going to ask. There was such an enormous pool of unspoken information and history and speculation between the two of them, and now this experience was another drop in the dark unyielding waters of that pool, which only received things, never gave them back.

Nick got on his bike without saying anything and started to ride. It was often like this when they used to go on their biking expeditions. Nick would start to go somewhere and Alex would follow, the two of them moving in silent tandem for hours. Sometimes Alex would move to the front and lead for a while, then they would switch back.

Nick began to move up Eighth Avenue very fast. As bike messengers, both of them had prided themselves on their speed and recklessness, and now, approaching fifteen, Alex was starting to lose some of his fat and he delighted in keeping pace with Nick as they sped uptown, the illuminated statue of Columbus looming grandly in the distance. When they reached it Nick made a sharp right, and headed east. Together they made their way past the hotels on Central Park South with their brightly lit entrances and rows of mangy horses attached to old-fashioned carriages out front. They slowed down to watch a large white horse lift its tail and crap majestically right in front of the Plaza. At Fifth Avenue they turned right again, and headed south. Not a word was spoken. They biked down Fifth Avenue until there was no Fifth Avenue left and they were standing in front of the arch in Washington Square Park, towering and white, like the entrance to a kingdom. At Nick's suggestion, they each bought two beers and sat on a bench in the park. That the grocer didn't say a word when presented with the order made perfect sense that night.

"This is so great," said Alex, sitting on the bench. "We're alone. We're just out in the world."

"Yeah," said Nick. "We're just hanging."

They sat for a while in silence, each sipping his can of beer, observing the scene around them. Someone was playing a radio. Several people congregated in the empty fountain at the center of the park, talking. Nearby a man was playing a melodramatic version of "Yesterday" by the Beatles while some people passed a joint. Individuals milled around aimlessly. It was a world without mothers, where people floated about in a strangely untethered state.

At that moment, in two separate buildings uptown, two mothers talked on the phone in the flat matter-of-fact tone of detectives as they pored over a class list, deciding who would call whom at this time of night. They both focused on the moment, some time in the near future, when they expected their anxiety to dissolve into relief and the pleasing catharsis of anger.

Nick and Alex sipped their beers until they were empty, and then sat for a while longer, taking in the scene around them. Eventually they biked uptown through the unusually empty streets, past the street sweepers and the huge green garbage trucks, yawning and groaning like dinosaurs. Then, without a word exchanged, they coasted to a stop to watch as a group of men busily carried bundles of something colorful from a truck through the wide doors of a brightly lit store at Twenty-seventh Street and Sixth Avenue, the only store open on the otherwise shuttered block. Above the door a large sign read: FLOWERS.

"Damn, this early delivery is killing me!" one of the men muttered as he heaved something onto his shoulder. The store radiated light and color. Slowly, Alex and Nick drew closer to see what was happening—they drew closer and closer until they were inside the store with their bikes, surrounded by freshly cut flowers in heaps; it was a scene completely out of proportion to the neat bundles of cut flowers that sat politely in flower shops. Huge wooden crates filled with crushed ice lay around like open coffins, enormous bundles of flowers inside. There were white roses and yellow roses and pink roses but most of all there were red roses. The room bustled with activity, but no one acknowledged them. There was a strange logic to the moment: the middle of the night, flowers, two kids on bikes, wooden crates filled with ice.

"Fucking A," said Nick.

A relay of men with thick gloves moved past them, enormous bushels of carnations and roses and lilies slung over their shoulders like corpses, the heads dangling down. The light in the room was sharp and white. The air was cool and thick with smell. It smelled like the beginning of all things.

"Excuse me, pal," said a man with a clipboard. "Can I help you?

"Hey, Alex," said Nick. "We've got to go."

"Pal," said the man, "these aren't for sale."

Alex stared, transfixed, into the sea of flowers.

"Pal!" The man said again.

They rolled their bikes out onto the sidewalk.

"I'd like to swim in those," said Nick. "Just jump in and swim through the roses and stuff."

"Yeah," said Alex. "Just drown in it. Just dive in so it's nothing but red."

They started uptown on their bikes through the dark benevolent night. At Thirty-fourth Street there was a red light. Like most bike messengers, they played the game whose object was to keep your feet off the ground, moving in a slow tight circle until the light changed. They did this, first making two individual circles and then joining into one; a compact little dance, front and back wheels almost touching as they went around, slower and slower until they were almost still.

NONDESTRUCTIVE TESTING

ONE DAY Will arrived at work to find a new receptionist sitting behind the front desk, and all that morning he found himself contemplating his brief glimpse of her. She was a large woman, not just in size but also in the boldness of her features—her eyes were big and blue, her cheeks were daubed with bright rouge, her lips were red and full. Moving from his desk to the bathroom and back, Will showered her with glances, but offered just a flicker of a smile.

More than a mere convenience, the office bathroom was a sanctuary for Will. He would sit down in one of the stalls, rest his head in his arms, and listen to the quiet groaning of the skyscraper's plumbing. It was a very modern building on Fifty-second Street, a thin streak of black poking aggressively into the sky. On stormy days Will sat for long periods of time and listened to it sway.

Will worked at a bank, in a small esoteric subdivision which monitored the activities of other banks. He was a permanent temp, a condition that suited him, as this was not his intended career. He had just dropped out of divinity school at Yale when he took the job, and he was only going to keep it until he could figure out what he was going to do next. Gradually, however, what he was doing now and what he was going to do next merged into the same thing. His job was similar to that of a monk copying scripture by hand, except in this case what he was copying was loan agreements acquired by some sleight of hand from another bank. The purpose of copying the information—which had been acquired on computer printout—in longhand was to give the appearance of research, not theft. It was supposed to take six months. A year had passed, and no end was in sight. The corporate salesmen in the office had caught his eye. They were cheerful energetic men in well-tailored suits whose arrivals and departures were always accompanied by great flurries of activity, and he felt a twinge of admiration for them. Something crass and materialistic was stirring within him, and he vaguely enjoyed the thought that it might be his fate to be rich, to be a mover and shaker, a man of surfaces.

His reasons for dropping out of divinity school were complicated, and he had a hard time explaining them to the many people who were confused and concerned by his decision, including his girlfriend, Liza, who shortly thereafter became his ex-girlfriend. The best analogy he could come up with was that of a musician who is suddenly gripped by performance anxiety and no longer wants to play his instrument before an audience—the audience in this case being God. In fact, he had come to the private conclusion that there was no audience.

All morning a parade of people came in and out of the office, most of them welcoming the new receptionist warmly, some just nodding. If someone got a call and wasn't at his or her desk, she got to page the person over the office intercom. Every few minutes she would have her own mini-performance for an audience of about fifty. Several fashion magazines lay on her desk alongside a bulky copy of the score of *La Traviata*. She was looking at one of the magazines when she first met Will, who was returning from yet another trip to the men's room.

"Did I get any calls just now?" he said brusquely.

"Um, you're . . ."

"Will. Hi." He smiled for a moment.

"No, no calls, Will." His name came off her tongue with something approaching familiarity. She spoke slowly and her words had just a hint of a Southern accent around the edges.

"Oh," he said, staring at her thoughtfully. "Good." He was of medium build with dark hair and thin black eyebrows that were just slightly askance, giving him a perpetually expectant look.

"Well, Will," she said. "I'm Marla. And how are you doing today?"

"Fine," he said and then added, "Bored. Extremely bored. I can't even tell you."

"You don't have to," she said. "What I'm doing isn't exactly fascinating either. But"—and here she sighed in a somewhat dramatic manner—"it gets me through school."

"School?" he said, raising his eyebrows as though it was a piece of slang he hadn't yet heard.

"I'm here to study opera at the Juilliard School," she said brightly. "I've already performed down in Austin, where I'm from."

Something about her enthusiasm embarrassed him—suddenly he was very self-conscious of his hands. "That's nice," he said, and turned to go back into the office.

"Seen the new receptionist?" Will said to his coworker, Hoffman.

Their desks faced each other in a small fluorescent-lit room. The vice president in charge of the division—a loud over-friendly man whose ambition was as evident as a dog's lust while it humps someone's leg—had come up with what he considered a snappy title for their project: "Info-War." Among the two soldiers, however, moral was low.

"Yup. Saw her," said Hoffman, and didn't move his eyes from the page in front of him.

"She's really quite, you know . . ." Will paused, trying to figure out just what word he was looking for. "Nice," he said finally, though this wasn't what he meant. "Nice" was the word for everyone else in the office, the kind of "Let's just be nice to one another so we can get through this damn situation, all right?" brand of friendliness that Will despised. Marla was something else. "She's an opera singer," he said. "Did you know that? And from Texas. An aspiring opera star from Texas."

When Hoffman made no response, Will stared at him, at the clean creases of his dress shirt, the tight knot of his tie and the miraculous dimple it created just below, which, despite hours of rehearsal in front of a mirror, Will had not been able to duplicate. Hoffman was one of those men who seem to have been born with an innate understanding of how to choose a suit, how to knot a tie, how to walk around with a cool, hand-some expression that would be as appropriate for a office party as it would for foreclosing on a family farm. Will had taken great satisfaction in Hoffman's one discernible flaw: a skin problem of some sort on his right index finger, which left it dry and scaly and which had prompted the fingernail to attempt an evacuation. Will would stare at that finger, mesmerized as it made the small squiggly motion of handwriting, and imagine what internal terrors it represented.

It was the morning of Marla's arrival that Hoffman, with the air of someone involved in high-level espionage, announced his plans to leave the company and start his own business, a newsletter that reported on the nondestructive testing industry.

"I didn't know you could test destructively," said Will.

"Nondestructive testing is a way of testing things like airplanes and nuclear reactors without actually taking them apart, or trying to damage them to see if they hold up," said Hoffman. "It uses ultrasonic waves, infrared light, radiology, things like that. It's the testing of the future. There's no harm."

"Experiments with no risk," Will said. He liked the metaphysical possibilities for something like this. His life had been full of tests and experiments, and most of them, it seemed, had been fairly destructive. A year and a half earlier he had had a career and a girlfriend, for example, and now he had neither.

At three o'clock Will was seized with a desperate craving for something sweet. It was as instinctive as the odd habit he had of waking up one minute before his alarm went off every morning. He fiercely tried to resist, but to no avail, and every day he made a pilgrimage to the lobby newsstand to buy a candy bar. On his way out today, he paused, quite impulsively, in front of Marla.

"How're you doing?" he said, cheered by the sight of her. He caught himself in the ridiculous arabesque pose he sometimes affected when he was trying to imply that he had been up late the preceding night doing something fabulously interesting. He corrected himself immediately and stood up straight.

"Just fine," she said, and her voice filled the room. It was clear, friendly, melodious, and slightly melodramatic—the kind of voice that would be equally appropriate for the evening news or phone sex. All day he had been listening to it page people over the office intercom. He smiled at her.

She smiled back. Her skin was smooth and clear except for a faint birthmark just below her left temple, the color of a coffee stain.

He stood there struggling for something to say. After a few seconds he just nodded and turned to go downstairs for his candy bar. He rode down with an attractive woman whose prim constrained manner seemed like an active rebellion against her pretty features and full hips. In this regard she reminded him of Liza, who was always worried about her weight in spite of the fact she had a lovely figure. He had teased her that no matter how much weight she lost she would always have a nice juicy ass for everyone to see. He told her that he had been fat when he was younger, and she was so amused by this, and amazed, since he showed no signs of it now, that she started calling him Fatty, until he asked her very seriously to stop. He saw his early fatness as a kind of purgatory through which he had suffered, and the thought of what he had endured in grade school still made him shudder.

When he returned to the office, Marla was handling several calls at once. The switchboard was filled with blinking red lights. Her large fingers with their bright red nail polish poked at the tiny buttons, and her face had a look of confused concentration—the blank expression of the kid in a seventh-grade spelling bee who, when confronted with the word "friend," is stumped. He had been that kid. Her lips were slightly parted, red and glossy, turned down a bit at the corners.

He imagined something white and sticky splattering across that open mouth. The image arrived with such sudden intensity that he turned the corner into the office area with a slightly shocked look on his face, as though he had just stepped over a pornographic photo lying face up on the street.

The next day Will arrived in his usual morning stupor and flew past Marla with hardly a nod. He was late and the vice president had recently posted a letter in the office lunchroom that read: "I have noticed an increase in tardiness among the staff. THIS WILL STOP." Against all rationality, Will suspected the president was making a subliminal communication to him. On that particular day the vice president was in one of his hands-on, loiter-around-the-little-people moods, and so Will had to forgo his bathroom respites. He worked right through lunch. He couldn't get away until midafternoon, and by then he had completely forgotten about Marla. Her voice, normally so musical and intriguing to him when it wafted over the intercom, had become part of the background drone of the office.

When he saw her he came up short. She was wearing a very sharp two-piece jacket-and-skirt outfit with a checkered pattern, and a white dress shirt with some frills around the collar. Her light brown hair was pulled into a knoblike bun behind her head, and a few minor curls escaped around her neck. It was the Female Executive as Impersonated by Receptionist look.

"Hi there," she said. "Where've you been?"

"Drowning," he said.

"I didn't know there was a pool back there," she said. "I'll have to bring my bathing suit."

Will's mind, enfeebled by a grueling day, was not ready for this image. He abruptly turned and started to head for his candy bar. Then he had a strange impulse and turned around to face Marla.

"Do you have any candy?" he asked.

"Candy?" she said. He was about to turn away and head downstairs when her face performed one of its dramatic changes; it took on the expression of a shoplifter caught red-handed.

"Yes, I do," she said with a slightly confessional fervor, and started to rummage around the large leather bag that served as her purse. "Here." She held out a small white paper bag. "Take the whole thing. I don't want any. I shouldn't have even bought them."

Will walked over and took the bag from her. She seemed relieved to have it out of her hand. It was half full.

He looked at her with a slightly confused expression, not understanding her urgency.

"Really, please take it all, I shouldn't have even bought it."

In that short sentence Will found more emotion than in anything he had heard uttered at work in the year he had been there, and he found his sudden proximity to a human being at once exhilarating and distasteful. Inside the bag was a small cache of little coffee-bean-shaped chocolates. They were the sort of candy his grandmother used to have in a bowl on the coffee table when he came for a visit. They were bittersweet. They were refined.

"Coffee beans," he said, peering into the bag.

"They're good. They're much better than the Reese's Peanut Butter Cups and that sort of junk me and my roommate eat most of the time."

"I'll just take one," he said.

"No! Really, take the whole thing."

He took two and handed the bag back to her, pleased at this newfound ability to torture her.

"Thanks," he said. On the way down in the elevator he ate one; it tasted just as remembered, refined and discreet, bitter-sweet. He put the other one in his desk, and he glanced at it periodically, the way one might glance at a pebble taken from a beach long ago and remember the whole vacation.

The next day, on his way back from his snack errand, Will presented Marla with a present.

"I have something for you," he said and leaned against the wooden counter in front of her.

"You have something for me?" said Marla, and swung her chair around towards him, her voluptuous body performing a kind of twist while seated. Her shoulders and breasts came at him with alarming velocity; her face wore an expression of excited anticipation, as though she were thinking, "What a nice man," but it also had an element of mock surprise, the expression of an adult receiving a present from a little boy.

Their eyes met, and Will stared intently into hers as he swung his arm out from behind his back, a Hershey's chocolate bar sitting in the middle of his pink hand.

Marla bit her lower lip.

"With Almonds," he said.

"Oh," she said. "Thank you. That's nice of you."

"Just returning the favor."

"I shouldn't."

"I thought you liked chocolate?"

"I love chocolate," she said. "But I shouldn't."

Will almost said, "Why not?" but decided this was too cruel.

"Tell you what," he said. "I'll leave it here and you can eat it if you want." He put the chocolate bar down right in front of her, smiled, and walked back into his office without saying a word. When he came by later that afternoon it had disappeared. He peeked conspicuously at the place where he had left it and then at her.

"Thank you, Will," she said.

This turned into a daily ritual. Will would return from his snack errand and deposit a chocolate bar in front of Marla, who would protest vehemently.

"Don't, please don't," she would say. Or she would say, "You're spoiling me." And once: "You're only doing this because you know I can't resist."

A secretary watched the exchange and said, "How come you keep bringing her candy when she says she doesn't want any?"

Will shrugged. "Maybe she doesn't mean it," he said, to which the secretary responded with a disapproving look.

"Oh, he knows I love it," he heard Marla say as he walked away.

Outwardly, these exchanges resembled the polite empty cheerfulness that pervaded all the interactions in the office. Will liked that. The surface propriety rendered it a nonevent, an exchange that needn't have any consequences, and therefore what happened beneath the surface could go to the farthest extremes.

He imagined her onstage, her full, shapely body and naked

optimism the focus of everyone's attention, her mouth issuing a dramatic high-pitched note. It was a stark contrast to the constrained gestures her job required.

He reflected on his own days, their utter mindless monotony, and contrasted it to the summer after college, when divinity school had lain ahead of him. Divinity school had been like a glass elevator that never stopped on any floor, but kept ascending to the greatest heights and descending to the lowest depths and never any exit. But what had replaced it was a world without elevators, one sprawling single-story structure with no elevation or descent.

But Marla hadn't fully arrived in this structure. She had a certain drive, a willfulness, and he admired it, coveted it even, and at the same time, felt a desire to crush it that had strange sexual overtones. He debated whether his teasing of her was wrong. He had always liked being tantalized. When he was a kid, his family had always said a long grace before dinner, and though he had found it excruciating, it did—he had to admit—increase his enjoyment of the meal once it finally started. And divinity school was the ultimate tantalization—his gaze focused intently on something he would never see. So, he thought to himself, what was wrong with being the tantalizer for change? Anyway, he rationalized, it was just a game.

The content of their exchanges slowly evolved. The candy bars were supplemented with gum and other small presents, though it was always something sweet. It was their little secret. She complained to him about not being able to get up from her spot at the switchboard—"I have no mobility," was how she put it—and he asked her questions about growing up in Texas, about opera; he liked listening to her voice.

Her one opportunity for "mobility" came when she made one of several trips during the day from the front desk to the kitchen to refill her plastic Evian bottle with water from the kitchen tap. She tended to use the same bottle for a week at a time and by the end of the first day her red lipstick would have tinted the nozzle. For the rest of the week it sat next to her, its tip bright pink.

Her trip to the kitchen took her past the room where Will and Hoffman worked opposite each other. Will always attempted to look deeply engrossed when she came by. He didn't want Hoffman witnessing their interactions, and also, he liked the idea that what he was doing seemed important.

"You drink a lot of water," he said one day when she returned with a full bottle. Hoffman had stepped away from his desk. She paused next to him. It was the first time she was standing while he was sitting.

"I'd rather be drinking gin and tonics," she said. She wore that imperious, I'm-too-good-for-this-place expression he liked so much.

"That's my favorite drink," he said.

"We'll have to have one together sometime." As she said this she casually reached over and stroked Will's hair and part of his neck. It was a mixture of a loving caress and the kind of tousling one gives to a little boy after he's done a good deed. He leaned into it a little, and his eyes took a slow reflexive blink of pleasure, like a cat being petted.

Their eyes met, and Will smiled nervously. He'd never actually considered being with her in the real world. The office was an artificial bubble within which they could have their flirtation, and even that was mostly restricted to that transient space of the reception area. If he saw her outside this rigid context, all the rules would change. Everything would be out in the open, beyond his control. They would be together by choice, her presence next to him announcing a conscious sexual preference. He saw himself at a restaurant with her and imagined bumping into a casual acquaintance, perhaps someone from the office. And then, as if to demonstrate what it would be like, Hoffman returned with an amused look on his face. Will stared at him, preparing to hate him if he said something snide, but as soon as she walked away Hoffman put a large envelope on the desk and removed its contents with the gingerly care of a man defusing a bomb.

"I just got the logo design for my newsletter. What do you think?"

He held up a piece of glossy paper.

"The Nondestructive Tester," Will said out loud.

"Well?"

"It has a nice ring to it. *The Nondestructive Tester.* Could be a newsletter for high school teachers specializing in very nervous students."

"I think it speaks right to the client, right to the people who are doing the testing, who are going to want to know the information we provide."

Hoffman's eyes began to shine and his voice dipped in pitch. This was obviously a speech he was preparing. Will pictured him standing in front of an easel, pointer in hand, making a presentation. The attending businessmen would look at his charts with glazed eyes and then at him, thinking, "How the hell does that guy get his tie to dimple so perfectly?" There was something charming about Hoffman's secret plans. He was like a prisoner unfurling the blueprints of the jail.

"Tester," said Will, musing. "*Tester*. Sounds a bit like 'testicle.' *The Nondestructive Testicle:* a newsletter for today's compassionate man."

Hoffman glared at him and put the secret plans back in their envelope, where they would be retrieved when the time was right.

Shortly after Marla's proposition, Will began to withdraw. It was an impulsive reaction. He did not want this experiment to leave the realm of the hypothetical. He felt this was a deficiency in his personality, like someone who constantly goes to enormous lengths to get to the beach only to then not go in the water, but he did not question it. He survived his job on the premise that it was temporary; to involve himself with Marla would make it part of his life.

First the candy bars stopped, then the idle banter at the reception area, and finally he began to avoid her glances altogether. Marla reacted to each new development like a dancer who steps forward each time her partner steps away. Her voice was as smooth and rich as ever, but it began to be inflected with recrimination. She could pack the phrase "Good morning, Will" with enough information to make his hands moist. He felt the sting of her disappointment but could think of no course of action other than to hide from it. He occasionally caught her in an expression of wistfulness and felt that he had joined the enormous ranks of people in the world who didn't appreciate her. But his sympathetic feelings were entirely internal, and now he marched past her to the bathroom with hardly a nod, even as those visits had been transformed into brief convulsions of masturbatory pleasure, with her as the subject.

Then one day Marla walked past his desk and dropped a chocolate bar on it. "Returning the favor," she said, and then walked away.

When the phone rang, Will was in his underwear and socks, pacing around the living room with a gin and tonic. Rock music blared in the background; his work clothes lay crumpled in a chair. This was one of his primary forms of entertainment, having a drink by himself and playing music. It was early in the evening and he was slightly drunk.

"Will?" Marla's voice wafted over the phone into his ear. It had been nearly two months since she had started working at his company and several weeks since they had stopped talking. He cocked his head, paused, looked around his apartment. He didn't want to answer. There was something gross about her voice intruding into his home. Her voice was the official voice of the workplace.

"Will? Is that you? It's Marla. I'm down at this bar."

"Hold on," said Will, and went to turn the music off. "You're at a bar," he said when he returned.

"Yes. Just a few blocks away from you, as a matter of fact."

"How did you find out where I lived?"

"I have my ways." Her voice slurred a little, its Texas accent more pronounced than usual. "Would you like to come join me?"

A picture of her sitting alone at a bar came to him. He imagined what sort of man would try to pick her up. He wondered if this was something she did often, go to bars and get drunk by herself. Half of him wanted to run over and rescue her from what he was picturing and the other half wanted to slam the phone down in its cradle.

"Why don't you come over here?" he said instead. For a second he wanted to retract it, but it was too late. He listened to his words fly over the phone. "I've got some gin, some tonic . . ." Happy bar sounds gurgled over the phone like a running tap, but Marla was silent. "Some lime."

"Oh, well, if you have lime . . ."

She said she would be there in ten minutes.

Will put the phone down and stood still for a few moments.

"You're crazy," he announced to no one, and then without missing a beat he began to frantically run around the room cleaning up. Tiny gold beads were scattered around his apartment, the strange legacy of Liza's last visit, when her necklace broke. He kept thinking he had found the last one and then another would pop up. He saw one now, glimmering in the corner, and picked it up to examine it. It was like a germ of Liza's presence, and he was reminded of her faintly disapproving manner, the way that their sex life had, after an auspicious beginning, made a slow steady retreat into propriety and then nonexistence. But this was part of his past. He was free of it now, and with his newfound liberty he decided to do something extravagant and perverse. He was going to buy a chocolate cake. He was going to make Marla take off all her clothes and sit at the kitchen table with a napkin around her neck like a bib. It would come down to the tops of her breasts. Her nipples would bob in and out of sight, and he would feed her chocolate cake with his hands.

He put on his pants and was halfway out the door when he glimpsed his apartment in its disheveled state and was suddenly gripped with the desire to make it nice for Marla. He went back to neatening up.

The doorbell made him jump. He opened the door and she stood in the doorway, and for a fleeting moment she looked quite small. She was wearing the same outfit she had worn at work that day, a light green skirt and a black long-sleeve shirt with large fake jewels—blue, green, and red—sewn in around the neck. She stepped inside amidst an invisible cloud of fragrance, what seemed like an entire display counter's worth of perfume.

"It's nice," she said, looking around and taking a deep breath as though she'd just completed a long trip. "So much room!"

"Really? You must live in a closet."

"I do," she said. "And with a roommate."

Will had planned to escort Marla to the kitchen table, but Marla took matters into her own hands and walked over to the couch, which was old and in bad shape and which made a painful groaning sound when she sank into it.

Will stood nervously, as though he were a maître d' about to apologize for some terrible mistake.

"I was supposed to meet a friend but they never showed up," she said. "Aren't you going to make me a drink?"

Will slowly emerged from the shock of seeing Marla on his couch.

"Yes, yes, of course. Gin and tonic, with lime. I have ice." As he turned to go to the kitchen he thought he glimpsed a slight expression of anxiety on Marla's face. This was hard for her too, he thought, especially hard for her; she was in a strange person's house who hadn't been very clear about his intentions and who might even turn out to be unpleasant. Christ, he thought, we're both human beings. Why is it so hard to treat someone like a human being? Thinking these thoughts, he made the drinks, and as he returned to the living room he realized he had talked himself out of even the slightest drop of sexual desire.

She was on the couch, her large shapely body folded in on itself, her skirt riding up over her thighs, which were covered with dark nylons. She looked anxious and helpless, and he found this attractive.

"Here," he said, handing her a drink.

He eyed the spot next to her on the couch and then opted for the relative safety of a chair next to it.

"So," he said.

"Well," said Marla. "Your place is very nice."

"I didn't get a chance to clean it up or anything. Usually when I have company . . ."

"No, it's nice. Besides, you didn't really have much warning." She gave Will a polite smile which was open to several thousand possible interpretations. She twirled her glass around and the ice cubes clinked merrily. This gesture seemed very well rehearsed and for a moment she seemed completely composed, even powerful, like a television executive whose show was riding high on the charts.

Will gulped his drink. "It's weird to have you here," he said.

"Does it bother you?" she said. "I could just go."

"No, it doesn't bother me. It's just weird. I mean, I'm used to seeing you at work. It's like, I only know you in that context."

"Well, I don't like that context very much. It's just so boring. You're sick of it too."

"I arrived there sick of it and it's been getting worse every day," he said. "It got a little better when you showed up, though."

She smiled a shy flattered smile which made Will think about what she had been like growing up, before she acquired the monstrous feminine presence she now had. He wondered if her classmates made fun of her, if she had breasts when she was ten, if she was teased. She probably couldn't have been a cheerleader. He pictured her wearing one of those skimpy outfits, kicking her legs up and down out of time with the other cheerleaders, her pom-poms flying up and hitting her in the face.

"Were you a cheerleader?" he ventured. "You know, when you were in high school?"

"That's a strange question, Will. Why? Do I act like a cheerleader?"

"No, no, it's just, you know, Texas, high school football . . ."

"No, I wasn't a cheerleader." She sipped her drink. "I was in the marching band."

"Oh. Sort of a big jump from that to opera."

"My life is full of big jumps," she said.

"I'm glad you jumped to New York."

He leaned towards her, gulped his drink, and raked her body with his eyes.

Marla saw this and shifted her drink from one hand to the other. Her eyes narrowed but then opened as if she had just remembered something.

"Well, it was nice having you as one of my early friends. And I do emphasize *early,* since you seem to have lost your enthusiasm for it lately."

"I have?" said Will defensively. "What do you mean?"

136

"What do I mean?" she said with some volume. It dawned on Will that maybe she had come over to yell at him. He sat back in his chair.

"What do I mean?" she repeated. "I mean that one day you're buying me candy and hanging around and talking to me and the next day it's like I just offended your mother or something and you can hardly look at me."

"You didn't offend my mother," said Will, retreating into the literal as a defense.

"I know damn well I didn't offend your mother! So what did I do to make you so hostile all of a sudden?"

"I don't think the topic of my mother even came up."

Marla looked at him with exasperation. "Don't avoid the subject."

"What was the subject again? My mother?"

"Will!"

"Oh, was it *your* mother?"

"Will! Come on." Her voice softened a little and became small. "What did I do?"

"Well, you're here now, so what does it matter?" He stood up. "I need another drink. Can I get you one?"

She handed him her glass without saying anything.

When he returned he eyed the spot next to her on the couch but then returned to his chair.

"We don't even know each other," he said. "All I know about you is that you're from Austin and that you study opera and that you're going to be an opera diva or something. I don't even know much about opera. And you know even less about me. I wear a tie every day and work in a stupid office. You don't even know if I'm the president or some schlemiel in the back room."

"I'm sorry," said Marla, "but it's very obvious that you're a schlemiel in the back room."

He was amazed at how hurt he was by the statement of this simple fact, but he decided to ignore it.

"For all you know I could be a psychotic killer. I could be a pervert. You know how it is, the guys walking around in ties and suits all day being polite, they have years of accumulated weirdness inside of them waiting to explode."

"Don't flatter yourself. There's not much killer in you. As for being a pervert . . ." She paused, as though it wasn't out of the question.

"I could be a poet for all you know," he said, as if this was an even more horrifying prospect.

"Oh could you?" she said facetiously.

Will stared at her face. The coffee-stain birthmark throbbed just beneath her temple. He hadn't considered the possibility that she could be cruel too, and this possibility interested him. He spoke calmly. "What do you think is going on with me, anyway? Do you think I *want* to be mean to you?"

"No, Will," she said, quite softly. "I think you're nice. You probably think you're less nice than you really are. You probably like the idea of it. But you *are* nice. I just don't know why you stopped being nice to *me*."

Her insight was true, and in telling the truth she had exerted a form of power to which Will had no immediate response. He had made one tiny little experiment, a minor test, and the destruction was running rampant. It was out of his control. He tried to form a sentence but couldn't. And so—partly out of desire, partly because all other options had been exhausted—he lurched forward and pressed his lips against Marla's. They were

138

slippery with gin and lipstick, parted in surprise, soft and warm against his hard aggressive mouth.

She pulled back instinctively and pressed her hand against his chest, then relented a little, and his tongue found its way into her mouth for an awkward moment. Will remembered the confused look of concentration he had seen on her face that first day, with her full lips parted dumbly, and imagining that her face now had that same expression sent a surge of excitement through him. She pulled away just as he lunged forward in his desire, groping at her, and in one frantic moment everything slipped away from him, including his drink, which landed right in the middle of her lap.

"Will!" she screamed.

"Oh shit," he said, referring as much to his unexpected gesture as to the stain that stretched from her waist nearly to her knees. Several ice cubes sat stranded on the grayish-green fabric.

"Will!" she screamed again. "What's the matter with you!" She looked at him with wide incredulous eyes. "Go get me a towel, for Christ's sake!"

Will jumped off the couch and ran to the kitchen, returning with a clump of paper towels dangling from his outstretched arm like a bouquet of flowers.

"Here," he said. He watched as she attended to the wet spot with urgent, fussy energy. He stood over her for a moment, and then, feeling silly standing there, started pacing the room in a circle.

"What's the matter with you?" said Marla again. "Don't they *train* men in New York? Does someone take you out for a walk on a leash when you get home from work?"

She seems upset, thought Will. *"God,"* he said sarcastically. "It's not that big a deal."

"And then you probably come home and eat dinner out of a bowl on the floor," she went on. Her head was down and he thought he heard her voice crack. "You probably sleep on a pillow in a big wicker basket. You probably . . ."

"I didn't mean it," he said.

"I know just what you're thinking." Her voice lowered. She looked at him with narrow eyes. "Do you think this is news to me? You think you're a novelty? With your nervous stares, your little games."

"Oh shit," said Will, and he went into the bathroom, where he spent several minutes washing his face with cold water.

"I'm sorry about that," he said when he came out. "I'm just a little drunk."

"You're behaving awfully," she said. She was standing now, inspecting her skirt.

"You were the one who wanted to come over," he said, and immediately flinched because it sounded like a kid trying to get out of the blame for something. He didn't understand why he kept acting like a thirteen-year-old with this woman.

"Actually, I *accepted* your invitation. If you had said, 'Would you like to come over so I can maul you and spill my drink on you and then act unpleasantly,' I would have told you to fuck off."

"I'm sorry," he said.

"Is this how you normally relate to women?"

"No," he said. "I don't usually spill my drink on them." And then, "I must admit, you have a strange effect on me. I don't think I understand it."

They were standing several feet apart, facing each other, their bodies slightly taut as if they were in a martial arts class and one of them was about to execute a takedown. Just then Will glanced over at the window and noticed he had neglected to pull the shades down. Across the alley stood another building, ridiculously close to his, its face a crossword puzzle of light and dark squares. He wondered if they had had an audience for the entire encounter, and he considered how the scene might have looked from a distance, viewed without sound, like a silent movie.

"Look," he said, "we've been performing. You like that, don't you? We've had our own little tragedy."

"More like a farce," she said.

He walked over to the window and cupped his eyes against it so he could see out better. When he first moved into the apartment he had been horrified at how available other people's lives were to him, but after a while he grew to like it. He marveled at apartment buildings, at how lives could unfold in such proximity without ever touching; just then he could see a woman peeling potatoes in her kitchen for what seemed like a large meal; next to that, a couple curled up on their couch, bathed in the flickering blue light of an unseen television.

"I don't know what you're doing," said Marla, "but I'm leaving.'

"Wait!" said Will. "I'm casing the joint. You have to know who you're performing for. You're going to be a diva, right? A star. And stars love to perform. I've never heard you sing."

Marla looked at him with an irritated expression and picked up her purse. She took a few steps towards the door and turned to him, inhaled, and let out a single burst of sound, a single high note that elevated him off the floor for several seconds and then dropped him, weak-kneed, back on his feet. She walked out with an air of triumph, and let the door slam behind her. He stared at it for a long time, half expecting it to open again. When it didn't he went and made himself another drink. He decided on the spur of the moment to quit his job. He smiled weakly at the thought of telling the vice president. He was quite shaken up. A stranger looking in from across the alley could have seen it on his face.

A DIFFERENT KIND OF
IMPERFECTION

AND THEN it was Christmas vacation and he was home. "Welcome home, Alexander!" his mother said when he walked in the door, pressing her warm face against his cold one. She was the only person who used his full name. It sounded odd.

She had bought some flowers and arranged them around the house in the special way she had of making things seem nice and attended to. Having brought him up alone—his father had died when he was ten—his mother was diligent about respecting his privacy, not prying into his life. He always felt guilty about not wanting to tell her things about himself, the few times she asked. After all, he was her son, her only child, and his life would be of interest to her.

"So. Tell me about school," she said now, sitting across from him at the kitchen table. His bags were piled up behind him in the foyer and he slouched in his chair, which seemed too small for him. The whole house seemed oddly small in comparison to the high ceilings of the ancient dorm he lived in at Vassar, where he was now a sophomore.

The scene—he and his mother in the same chairs, the same look on her face—reminded him of coming home from kindergarten and having his mother and father ask him how school was, while they sat at the kitchen table. He had always shrugged and said nothing, but he sometimes wondered whether both of his parents had spent their entire day waiting for him at the kitchen table, discussing him. All that attention seemed to demand more from him than anything he could supply with meager details about his fractions or papier-mâché cow, and so he usually said nothing. Eventually he would shrug and slouch on into his room, down the long dark hallway. But he had always liked the idea that both his parents had been in conference over him all day.

Now here was his mother, sitting in the same position at the kitchen table, smiling and asking him the same questions, looking loving and a little daunting, as usual. It was too much love to live up to.

"There's really nothing much to say," he answered, thinking about Sloan, his suddenly ex-girlfriend. She lived in Baltimore. He had never thought about that city, but now that Sloan lived there, was in fact there that very moment, Baltimore seemed like an alluring place. "I seem to be getting the hang of how to be a college student," he said. "It's not too difficult."

"And your studies?"

Alex winced at the word. "Studies" was too dignified for what he was doing. "Well, I'm not going to major in sociology. That's all I can say for sure."

"What's it like?" she asked.

"The dorms are pretty nice, but at night the only place to get food is the candy machine." He paused for a moment. "The classes are good, though," he went on, thinking she would enjoy hearing that.

Sloan was the first girl he had really gone out with in college, and by extension, the first girl he had really broken up with. She was a vegetarian poet who had her own place off campus, which seemed like a very daring move in sophomore year. Her apartment was just across the road, but the fact that it was technically off campus made it seem illicit. They had gone out together for a few months, but just before vacation Sloan informed him—or "reminded" him, as she pointed out—that she had another boyfriend at home. She told him that she felt she had to give that a chance. It was shaping up to be a miserable Christmas vacation, he thought.

His mother cupped her face in her hands. Her chin rested on the heel of each palm and her fingers were over her cheeks, framing her face. She was very pretty, and yet her happiest expression always seemed to have a tinge of sadness. His father had died of cancer nine years earlier, and Alex couldn't remember whether this look of gravity had come into her face after that. Perhaps being happy always reminded her of her loss. She hadn't remarried. She hadn't even painted the apartment. Alex looked into her liquid eyes and smiled. Then he escaped down the hall.

His room seemed different. Freshman year, he had scurried down to New York from Poughkeepsie almost every chance he got, and his first Christmas vacation had seemed like a reprieve. His room had welcomed him. His mother had welcomed him. The whole house had burst to life, as if it had been in suspended animation since the day he left. Coming home this time was different; he couldn't get over how strange it felt to be back.

His room was just as he had left it, but it just sat there, inanimate, waiting to be occupied by whoever came along.

He went out into the early-evening light and walked over to a bar on Eighty-third and Amsterdam, the Jaunting Car. It was the last bar in his neighborhood with any charm, but today it was almost empty. He ordered a scotch and looked at himself in the mirror behind the bar. One of the better things he had acquired since going to college was a taste for scotch. Previously he had drunk only vodka, a habit he had formed at the age of fourteen when he had sampled all the bottles in his parents' liquor cabinet and had decided that vodka was the least unpleasant. His mother didn't drink, and hardly ever had guests, and it had sometimes occurred to him that the bottle of Wolfschmidt he was drinking from had probably been bought by his father. His first cigarette, which he had smoked at about the same age, had come from an ancient pack of Dunhills he had found in a table drawer, in among a collection of broken sunglasses frames, pipe cleaners, loose buttons, and other artifacts of his father's. It was an odd collection of items, the debris that comes together only because there isn't enough of any one thing to require its own drawer. When he came upon it, four years after his father had died, the stash itself looked static, stunned with age. That cigarette, Alex recalled now, had been rancid. The pack of Dunhills was probably still there. The drawer was always shut.

He spent the first few days back from school mostly alone. He had stopped frantically trying to touch base with friends from high school, the way he'd done at this time a year ago. He thought about Sloan, he walked around the streets at midday in the bright high winter sun, and spent hours meandering around his house examining shelves and closets he hadn't looked at in years. The apartment, with its cracked and peeling paint, its rickety wooden chairs with half-broken cane seats, was filled with books, among them many dark green or maroon volumes with titles like *Textbook of Pathology* and *Clinical Hematology,* and a huge book with the ominous title *Heart.* His father had been a doctor—a psychiatrist. Alex perused the bookshelves with a peculiar interest, as if he were looking for clues. One set of twenty-four books in pale blue dust jackets took up an entire shelf: the complete works of Sigmund Freud. He took out *Totem and Taboo* and looked at the first chapter, "The Horror of Incest." He put the book back with the haste of someone who had opened the door of an occupied bathroom.

Scanning for a lighter topic, he took out *Jokes and Their Relation to the Unconscious.* He opened to a random page and read, "It is remarkable how universally popular a smutty interchange of this kind is among the common people and how it unfailingly produces a cheerful mood."

He returned the book to its place, and listened to the silence of the house. He and his mother lived in an apartment building, but all their neighbors were quiet. While he was growing up, the only noisy person in the building had been himself—he had once bounced a rubber ball so incessantly that the downstairs neighbors had called the police. He then took to throwing water balloons out the window. He was so intrigued by the way the balloons shimmered—like Jell-O, he thought—in their flight to the ground that he always forgot to duck his head back in the window in time and soon he got caught. He and his mother were nearly evicted, she told him. Again and again as he prowled around the house now, he was struck by the evidence of lives lived. It lay on the shelves, along the walls, stacked in piles on the floor.

Alex's college roommate, Milo, called and announced he was going to be in New York for an afternoon before he went skiing. They met in a coffee shop for lunch.

"You're bored," Milo said over a tuna fish sandwich. "You should get out of New York. Come skiing with me."

"I don't ski," Alex said.

"Come for the scenery."

"There's plenty of scenery here. I can see a little sliver of the Hudson River and part of New Jersey from my window."

Milo gave Alex an appraising look. "Come for the women," he said. "This place is going to be crawling with women. You need a distraction."

"I am distracted," said Alex. "I need to concentrate."

"You're concentrating on your distraction," Milo said. A little piece of food had lodged itself at the corner of his mouth. This completely discredited him in Alex's mind. The guy couldn't swallow properly; he wasn't someone whose advice was going to be helpful.

"All right, all right," Milo went on. "You're concentrating on Sloan, which is depressing you. Tell you what—work on it, and when you've got it perfected, give me a call." Then he neatly pinched the tuna speck from the corner of his mouth and flicked it at Alex.

"That was the problem with you and Sloan," he went on, with some satisfaction. "You were just an amateur at being depressed. Sloan was a pro. You couldn't keep up."

The apartment's foreignness had begun to wear off, giving way to something even more disturbing. It was familiarity, but not the kind that makes things disappear into the background. Now every detail jumped out and announced itself as significant, the way banal things became significant whenever there were guests in the apartment. Alex was his own guest now, he decided, a sightseer in his own home.

He began to realize that his house was submerged in books—hundreds and hundreds of them, in the corner bookshelf, on the bookshelf against the wall, or stacked in dusty heaps in a corner, spilling over everywhere. He noticed that some of the books held slivers of paper, which projected above the tops of the pages. He opened one such book and discovered faded pencil underlinings on each of the marked pages, with a word or two of comment here and there in the margin. Alex didn't know much about his father's intellectual life, but he had lately noticed that his father's haphazard handwriting bore a conspicuous resemblance to his own. He examined the pages more carefully, and the marginal notes seemed to confirm it. He went from book to book and eventually stopped at one and began to read. It was *To the Lighthouse* by Virginia Woolf—a book he'd never read.

The volume itself was old; its gray cloth cover was tattered at the corners, but the binding remained stiff and dignified. The pages were only slightly yellow and had a certain weight to them. The book had been published in 1927, five years after his father was born.

When had his father read it? He had arrived in America as a teenager sometime before the Second World War. So if he had read this in college, it would have been the early 1940s, and he would have been almost the same age as Alex was now, reading the same pages. But there was the possibility that he had read the book years later. Maybe even after Alex was born. There were no marks to indicate which, one way or the other.

He read on, turning each page in anticipation of another one of his father's marks. On page 99, a strand of pencil underlined a fragment of a sentence: ". . . she had known happiness, exquisite happiness, intense happiness . . ." It was not a line that would have jumped off the page at Alex, but seeing it underlined by his father disturbed him and moved him. The words "exquisite happiness, intense happiness" resonated above the whispery pencil mark that flowed underneath them. Alex stared at the pencil lines for a moment, as if they were completely separated from the writing. He was waiting for the lines to reveal something. The pencil was neither sharp nor dull. The lines didn't seem to have been drawn with a great deal of pressure, but they weren't too light, either. Had they been made in bed, or at a desk, or an armchair—or on a bus? He felt a pang of frustration, trying to imagine what his father had been thinking. It was a sharp twinge that made him shudder for a moment.

He was in the kitchen one afternoon, staring into the refrigerator, when his mother came in and sat down at the table expectantly, as if she wanted to have a conversation. He obliged, sitting down across from her.

She smiled, tilted her head a little, and said, "What are you thinking?"

"Nothing," he said. He wanted to say more but couldn't. It was always this way with his mother—the unwilling retreat.

"You have been walking around with a funny expression, as though something is bothering you."

"Nothing is bothering me, it's just odd to be back. You know, like, when you go away and then come back and it's, like—"

"Stop saying 'like.' "

"It's weird, then."

"I can tell something is on your mind. You have this cloudy look about you. I've been wanting to bring it up for some time now."

"I've only been home for three days."

"But before even. I've been worried about you." His mother had the rare but unmistakable expression she got when she was preparing to try to exert authority. She wasn't the authoritarian type, but in the absence of a father she had to take the offensive periodically.

"You seem very unfocused," she said. "As if you're drifting. There is a certain urgency lacking."

"What is there to be urgent about, Mom? It's Christmas vacation."

She looked at him some more, with her hazel eyes, which sometimes turned green. Her affection was discomforting, though he had never been without it, or even considered that he might ever be. He felt his cheeks warm up, and watched the corners of her mouth slowly turn into a bittersweet smile, as if she was seeing something that had not yet come into view for him.

Another passage read: "He knew, of course he knew, that she loved him. He could not deny it. And smiling she looked out the window and said (thinking to herself, nothing on earth can equal this happiness)—" A dried piece of scraggly orangish paper—a ripped strip of it—had stuck out of the top of the book like a buoy in a channel, and when he got to it he found these words underlined in pencil.

He took out the shred of paper and examined it. He was sitting on the floor in a dusty corner of the study, next to a ragged brown armchair. It was a shred, all right—one of several torn up and placed, perhaps, in a pile, so they could be used over the course of a reading session. This shred was the first of several sprouting up from the top of the book, a grove of markers densely clustered in an area where his father seemed to have found interesting material.

The next marked page contained just one underlined sentence: "It's almost too dark to see." Very enigmatic observation, thought Alex.

Some lines were neatly drawn, but most had been made casually, almost sloppily, though they never ran over the words. They wavered. It was hard for him to gauge how much the pencil marks had faded over time.

The whole issue of time and dates bothered him. How old had his father been when he made these marks? Alex wanted to know. Another underlined segment he came across was itself in quotes and read: " 'And all the lives we ever lived / and all the lives to be / are full of trees and changing leaves.' " How old would the man be who marked that?

He walked around his neighborhood in the daytime, looking at people passing, and wondering why they weren't at work. No one in the middle of the day in a residential neighborhood was in a rush, he realized. He scrutinized faces, searching for the anxiety of lateness, but only found people drifting into hardware stores, clothing stores, the corner market. What was their excuse? He had his and it comforted him: he was a student.

Such an easy excuse—he wondered how long it would last. At this rate, he thought, an eternity.

He imagined calling Sloan. "I've discovered peeling paint on all the walls and I've walked around the apartment pulling pieces off the ceiling so it won't look as bad," he would say. "The house hasn't been painted since three years before my dad died."

"Maybe you should get the place painted," she would say. She was annoyingly pragmatic when she wanted to keep a distance between them.

"I thought maybe you weren't having a good time with what's-his-name and wanted to come up to New York," he would say. He imagined what she would say to a question like that. He decided he wouldn't want to hear it.

Amid a battalion of small photographs set up on his mother's bedroom bureau was a small snapshot of his parents. His father and mother were extremely good-looking—particularly his mother, who had high sharp cheekbones and thin lips and wore her brown hair in a bun. Her family was from Berlin; her grandfather had been an enormously wealthy banker who had shot himself just after the First World War, when he had lost all his money. Alex liked that detail of his family history; the combination of death and money had a certain glamour for him.

His father had been born in Vienna. He was handsome in the photograph, with dark hair and deep grooves in his face, particularly in the forehead. He had a certain monkey quality to him. The picture was a head-and-shoulders shot of the two of them, dressed up nicely, with their shoulders squared to the camera but their heads turned a little toward each other, each of them gazing at the other's face. His mother looked stunning.

She was wearing a black dress that contrasted sharply with the string of pearls around her neck; her smooth skin caught the light and glowed. His father was merely handsome in comparison, and his smile suggested that he felt even gleeful at his good luck. But they shared a conspiratorial gaze, glimmering with hidden knowledge. Was it the secret of beauty? Was it the secret of happiness? Alex imagined the moment as intense.

The picture was small, not more than two inches square. His mother liked antique things, small things—frames and cameos in particular. The family history was suffused in a nineteenth-century ambience, completed by ornate silver embellishments and delicate wood carvings around the frames. The frames were precious, personal. He rarely saw them, though. Because of the sharp rays of the morning sun that flooded his mother's window, the pictures were all turned to face the wall. She had never managed to put up any blinds.

That the sun was fading the pictures was a discovery his mother had made somewhat late in the game, and most of the pictures had already lost a good deal of clarity, as if they were undergoing the development process in reverse. In one, he himself was walking on unsteady legs across the grass. He was chubby-cheeked but had a look of great purpose. But the photograph was now nearly a mirage, it had faded so badly.

His parents' good looks interested him, but not as much as their shared expression in the small picture. They had recently married. That was for sure. He was rugged and dark, and wise-looking, with his lined face. His mother looked like a goddess. Her eyes and his seared into each other's with deep meaning. Or was it just lust?

"Exquisite happiness, intense happiness." He looked at the words and then the scrawny pencil lines underneath them. The underlining was no more or less emphatic than elsewhere, but he still stared at it, trying to infer something more. When did his father read this? When did he make these marks? What was the proximity of the time of these marks to that of the small picture? To all the pictures? The day Alex had gone to the bureau and, in a rout of the established order, about-faced the whole group of photographs so he could look at them together, it had dawned on him that all the photographs of his father had been taken when he was an adult. He had reached a watershed in life that Alex had yet to get near. He had the look of a man whose twenties had never taken place, or, if they had, had somehow been lost. Where had his father been when he was twenty? What secrets had he learned between twenty and the time of the picture? What had prompted him to underline these words? What had he figured out?

An impossibility, an immovable wall, lay between Alex and the answer. He felt the strain of permanence in the situation and in everything that reminded him of it: the remaining cigarettes, the same paint on the walls, the stain on the headboard on his father's side of the bed. There was a secret in them that had clearly been lost. Gone down, away. It had descended beneath an impenetrable surface. Alex could only run his hands over it, searching for a subtle suggestion, a different kind of imperfection. He didn't feel sentimental about it. Just frustrated, like an archaeologist who has hit bedrock—no farther to dig. No more options. Except, perhaps, one. He decided to move laterally.

He began to scavenge the house for things obsolete, unexpected. He took a pack of the old, yellowed cigarettes and marched out into the day with it. Broadway glistened in the stunning white light of noon. It had been remarkably clear weather since he got back. Walking down the street with an ancient and unlit cigarette between his fingers, it occurred to him that he wasn't depressed at all. If anything, he was buoyant. He had this thing, this business about his father and his secrets of happiness, that he couldn't figure out. The challenge was dredging him up out of his self-pity about Sloan, and he took this to be a good sign.

He wasn't depressed—he was merely mystified. He was looking for something between the lines. Enjoying this state, he lit the cigarette and took a few lung-scorching puffs. Awful. He held it between his thumb and index finger, felt its warmth. He liked it in his hand. It was his father's cigarette—one of the last few in a pack that he had never had a chance to smoke. They'd been stranded.

Alex was reading *To the Lighthouse* with a dual diligence. He was watching for his father's markings but at the same time the book was captivating him in its rhythm, like a boat that rocks subtly, and whose rocking sensation persists even when its passengers have disembarked.

Then on page 193, he made a starling discovery. Between the pages he found a business card. Clearly meant as a marker, it had slipped down, so it hadn't been visible. The card was yellowed, and on it was his father's name, "Solomon Fader, M.D." In the lower right-hand corner was his father's office address and telephone number, with the exchange spelled out: "TRafalgar 9-3072." Alex picked up the card and turned it over in his hand for a moment before realizing the full significance of the find. His father was at that office for only the last nine years of his life. It meant that he probably knew he was dying as he read *To the Lighthouse,* for his illness, Alex knew, had lasted more than eight years.

Alex suddenly thought about a spring walk in Central Park that his mother had once told him about. The day was warm and sunny and his parents had gone out for a stroll at lunchtime. Things were going well for them, by any standard. Except during that particular walk the man in the picture informed his wife that he was dying, and things were no longer going well. By any standard. The words "She had known happiness, exquisite happiness, intense happiness" sprang to Alex's mind again. Then came the image in the photograph—that secret but happy gaze his parents shared.

Did his father read the book just before he found out he was dying of cancer, when things were going so well? When he had a career and a wife and a baby boy—or just after, when all such perceptions would be influenced by this new knowledge? Or had dying caused some kind of purified state of emotion, something that heightened everything? Was imminent death a magnifying glass through which the heat of life was intensified—enlarged and sharpened into a prism point of misery and joy?

He went out again and walked down the street, preoccupied with his thoughts. His gaze was fixed on the pavement in front of him. Then he lifted his head and saw his mother just down the block. She was holding a plastic grocery bag, but it was a light load, probably only a carton of milk, maybe some oranges, some bread. His mother, when not in a celebratory mood, lived frugally.

But it was her expression that stopped him. She too was engrossed in something, and had her head down as she scrutinized the ground in front of her. Her face looked concerned, even old, and it struck him that his mother was aging. Not that the idea was such a shock, but it jarred him to see how different the face he was looking at just then was from the taut, angular, smooth-skinned face that looked so coolly into the smiling monkeyface of his father, in the photograph. This face—her face now—wore an expression of mild confusion, as if she were trying to remember where she had left her keys.

He stood still as she approached him on a direct collision course. She was oblivious. The face that had so often warmed his looked a little gray. It came nearer, a visage, and only when she was only five or ten feet away did she look up abruptly, as if she had noticed his shoes standing still on the pavement. Alex had been smiling as she came nearer, and he was looking forward to the prospect of surprising her. But when she suddenly looked up, she had such an expression of alarm and shock that he felt his own face freeze. Her expression was completely unfamiliar. She was wholly surprised, off guard. Her mouth was slightly ajar, her eyes wide, her face a little slack around the edges. She blinked a moment, composing herself, registering that this was her son in front of her, and then started to smile.

But it was too late; he was upon her, hugging her. Something had come over him at the sight of her disorientation and he had leapt forward to embrace her, as if he were catching her in midfall. The leap was urgent—desperate even—and when he got to her he put his arms around her and squeezed her tightly to his chest, as if he were afraid that she might drop something or lose something, or as if some secret which only she knew would slip away.

SEDUCTION THEORY

T HE SUN HAD SET hours ago, but only now did the heat show
signs of relenting. Mark lay on his bed and thought, "This
must stop, I must get up, I must talk to someone." All day he
had been in and out of bed, making brief attempts at entering
the melted world of a summer Sunday in New York, only to
retreat to the cool lethargy of his white sheets and the groaning
fan that sat like a cannon two feet from the bed, strafing his
body from head to toe.

It was the first of August, and the first of the month had the
highest number of public disturbances, he knew, because it
was when all the government assistance checks came, and were
cashed, and on hot nights such as this the police were especially
busy. Lawless behavior was Mark's specialty—he was the managing editor of Arrow Publications, a company whose three
titles were *Master Detective*, *True Detective*, and *Inside Detective*.
Arrow had been faithfully chronicling lurid crimes since 1924.
There were only two criteria for a story to qualify: the crime
must be solved, and the story must be told from the point of
view of the detective. Thus: *Inside Detective*. The job had ini-

tially evoked images of Raymond Chandler and Mickey
Spillane, an atmosphere greatly enhanced by the presence of
Mr. Riley, the white-haired crank who had been piloting the
magazines for forty years and spent his days chewing the stub
of an unlit cigar and grousing about the ever declining quality
of crime.

Mark had initially seen Riley as a mythical figure, but recently
he had begun to seem pathetic in his nostalgia and bitterness, a
worrisome foreshadowing of the effects of too much time spent
reading and writing about kidnappings and revenge killings.
As Mark's affection for Riley declined, so did the appeal of the
job. It had been a wild idea at first, something that invariably
went over well at parties, something rebellious and unusual,
but now it was his profession, and its substance was a universe
of small acts of cruelty and violence. He passed his days in the
dim disheveled offices of a company whose heyday was decades
past, and just last week one of his coworkers had been offered a
producer's position on a successful television crime show at an
enormous salary. He felt the grip of circumstance closing
around him. He wanted out of crime. The heat only made
palpable a more interior desire for a change, something new
and unexpected.

At ten in the evening, quite suddenly and out of the blue, he
thought of Kate Doblin. They had met at a party nearly a year
ago, and he had taken her number and invited her to a party
he threw a few months later. When she had arrived that evening he was struck by something remarkable about her that he
hadn't noticed the first time—she was beautiful, but it was a
nervous beauty, a strange impulsive kind of beauty, and her
features kept going out of sync, tiny imperceptible tugs that,

had they been more pronounced, might have seemed like out-right twitches, but instead gave her a strange energized quality, something at once open and unpredictable.

Subsequently they had had a number of long phone conversations—she talking about her graduate studies in theater design, he talking about what strange things had crossed his desk that week or the general anxiety in his office that the magazines were being made obsolete by the television shows. They had attempted several get-togethers, but had never managed one. He always called at the last minute, as he was doing now.

"Not another spur-of-the-moment thing," she said when he announced himself. She sounded pleased to hear from him, though.

"In fact, yes. We could do any number of things, varying in extravagance," he said.

"Such as?"

"Starting at the top, we could go to a cold dark place and sit next to each other." He mentioned a movie, but she'd seen it. "Then there's dinner," he went on.

"I've eaten," she said. "Most people have by ten at night." Something in her voice seemed pleasingly receptive, as if her stand-offishness was a game. He liked games.

"And finally, at the bottom, drinks. I could come to your neighborhood."

"Really?" she said.

"Where is your neighborhood again?"

She reminded him of where she lived, a huge housing complex near Columbia University called International House. "There's a pub right in the building," she said. "You could come visit and we could have beers."

The evening, which had been so bleak and lifeless moments before, took on a terrific radiance. Suddenly there was the possibility of something interesting and entertaining, perhaps sexual. They might even get along.

International House occupied a strange corner of the city; it was an enormous structure on Riverside Drive and 122nd Street, built in 1924 and able to accommodate seven hundred residents. It bordered Harlem and Columbia University and the Hudson River, but stood apart from all these places, above them, on a steep hill. Most of its residents were foreign graduate students attending Columbia University, though many of the people who lived there, including Kate, were from another kind of foreign country, the Midwest. She was in her second year of the theater design program, which she had begun the autumn after finishing college; she had gone into the field partly because it sincerely interested her, and partly because she wanted to be involved in the theater but didn't want to lead the tenuous life of an actor or director. She was a romantic with a hard nugget of pragmatism lodged deep within her.

She had moved directly to International House upon arriving in New York and had lived there ever since. New York was thrilling but a bit overwhelming, and she found it comforting to have a self-contained place to which she could return from her adventures; the violence and strangeness of the city took place outside the building. She liked going to the pub downstairs in shorts and clogs in the middle of winter and knowing that there would be someone to talk to. And then there were the familiar faces and the low-intensity friendships that abounded, any one of which held the possibility of blooming into something more substantial. In fact, all of her romantic involvements since she had been in New York had been with International House residents, and even though this provided for an ample number of awkward moments, she didn't mind; it made her feel as though her life was within reach and available to her.

She met Mark in the fluorescent-lit lobby, amidst the machines selling soda and candy and cans of ravioli, next to the mailboxes. The main entrance on Riverside Drive was rarely used, and most of the residents came and went from a small rear doorway on Claremont Avenue composed of two narrow glass doors through which you had to be buzzed by a security guard, one at a time. She always considered the small space in between the doors to be a kind of decompression chamber, a neutral space, and now she saw Mark pause there, briefly suspended between her world and the one beyond.

Mark entered the lobby looking buoyant and lanky and a little pleased with himself, which is just as she remembered him—gleaming eyes, dark hair, and an upper lip which curved nicely. He was wearing shorts, and his smug and handsome face contrasted oddly with his knobby knees and narrow shins. For a moment she regretted the black silk scarf she had flung around her neck, but then she observed a transparent expression of lust and admiration cross his face when he saw her—an observation which was confirmed by the brisk and somewhat anxious kiss he planted on her cheek—and she was suddenly in a very good mood.

"I feel like I'm visiting a juvenile delinquent here," he said. "Can you leave on your own or do you have get special permission?"

"I can never leave. That's why you had to come here." She began walking him around the complicated system of hallways and staircases that led to various common areas, elegant rooms with high ceilings and functional-looking couches positioned against the walls.

"Am I going to be inspected by a tribunal to see if I'm proper date material for a resident of International House?" he asked.

"Is that what this is, a date?"

"Absolutely, an incredibly hot date," he said.

"What constitutes a hot date?"

"When you visit someone in the middle of the night for a beer." He smiled at her, and she smiled back, guardedly. His mouth, she thought, was perhaps the sexiest part of his whole body. His lips were at once full and slightly taut; sometimes he would press them together to form a tight line, a nervous habit she found attractive for some reason. He did this now.

"We might even have two beers," she said.

The pub was neither stylish nor sleazy, just a generic college pub, but he almost leapt in disgust as soon as he walked through its entrance.

"Here it is," said Kate, with remarkably genuine enthusiasm.

On the surface it was innocent enough: a large dim room with a makeshift bar in the middle, some tables off to one side, and a dance floor on the other. The song wafting through the room was perfectly poised at the midpoint between its initial popularity a few years earlier and its future career as kitsch favorite, which was several years down the road.

He thought to himself, "I hate this," and then, "What is my problem?" He was prone to fiercely snobbish assessments of things—pop songs, clothes, nightclubs, furniture—but was trying to ween himself from the impulse. His new credo was to be open-minded. He was going to be open to new experiences and stop pretending to be a connoisseur. If he was a connoisseur of anything it was of the vile and petty and lurid and, of course, the truth; all the criminals portrayed in *Inside Detective* were convicted and behind bars. The ending was always happy. Here was a new experience, and he vowed to be open to it.

He looked around the room again and noticed its remarkably diverse population: Indians and Hispanics and Asians and blacks and whites, chatting and drinking in different configurations.

"It's like that scene from *Star Wars*," he said, "where all those different creatures are congregated in a bar drinking steaming green cocktails and socializing. Then Han Solo gets into a fight, if I recall."

"Don't be mean," she said.

"I'm not. I like it. I feel like I'm on another planet."

She found a table while he stood at the bar waiting to order, and for a moment their eyes met and she smiled at him. It was an excruciatingly geeky moment, he thought. *"Look, honey, I'm at the bar . . . getting beers!"*

But then she lit a cigarette and, lips puckered, exhaled a thin stream of smoke at the ceiling. It was pretty. Then a man approached her; she greeted him with a broad smile and in a flash all her elegance was gone—she was a dumb girl who lived in a dormitory.

When he returned he found the man seated at their table.

"Mark this is Wayne, Wayne this is Mark," Kate said, and then added, "Mark and I are just having a beer."

165

Mark stuck out his hand but Wayne did not shake it. He just stared at him with eyes too narrow for the occasion, and a neck too thick with tension. He had the look of a man about to make a dare.

"Hello there," said Mark, his hand hanging in the air.

He was met with silence.

"I see we have one happy customer here," said Mark. He was competent at a kind of verbal jousting that was occasionally necessary when dealing with belligerent men, but his effectiveness in the art of confrontation dropped off quickly beyond a certain point. That point was the moment when words were no longer sufficient and it was time for one person to start hitting the other. "What's the matter?" he said, letting some contempt creep into his voice, like a poker player who is overbetting to conceal a weak hand. "The heat getting you down? Frustrated? Feeling a bit out of sorts?"

"So you're the *Inside Detective* guy, right?" said Wayne. "You spend a lot of time inside detectives?"

This comment threw him. Clearly there must be some relationship between Wayne and Kate for him to know this. Judging by his extremely unhappy manner, perhaps he was her boyfriend. This saddened Mark. But then again, judging from his extremely unhappy manner, perhaps he was her ex-boyfriend. This would have appealed to him, for purely dramatic purposes, except that Wayne was being unpleasant in a manner which suggested further unpleasantness to come.

"Have we met?" said Mark.

"You think you're something special, right?" said Wayne. "You think you're hot stuff, don't you."

"Actually my self-esteem fluctuates on an hour-to-hour basis," said Mark.

"You know what? You're an asshole. You're nobody. You're nothing."

"Thank you!" said Mark, his voice several octaves above its normal pitch. The intended sarcasm was diminished by the prepubescent delivery. He turned to Kate, who was dragging on her cigarette with incredible force. "Should I leave the two of you alone?"

She exhaled a huge cloud of smoke through her nose, which gave her the authority of an extremely annoyed dragon. "No!" she said with wide eyes. "Wayne, what's the matter with you? Behave yourself!"

There was a moment of silence at the table. Mark frantically sized Wayne up to see if a fight was practical. The initial evidence did not look promising. Wayne wasn't very tall, but his chest was broad and deep and his arms had the bulky look of someone who worked out regularly with weights. Mark was fairly big himself, but it was the wrong kind of big for fights. His limbs were long and his center of gravity was too high. He had been in fights, but his enjoyment of them was severely hindered by a deep instinctive desire to not be hit in the face. Now he sat waiting quietly to see what would happen.

After a moment Wayne said, "I'm sorry about that, I've got exams coming up and everything." He extended his hand, and Mark, after a moment's hesitation, took it. "I'm just a little tense."

"Wayne is going to be a star lawyer and give everyone on the hall free legal advice for the rest of our lives," said Kate.

What followed was several minutes of small talk. It was difficult for Mark to join in; he felt manipulated; Wayne had slapped him and now social convention was denying him his right to find a large heavy object and crash it repeatedly into

Wayne's skull. He trembled slightly, his anger and disgust covering everything in sight: the bar, its merry foreign population, Wayne, Kate, himself.

He gathered that Wayne lived down the hall from her. Mark had been out of college seven years and considered his career of running around dorm hallways to be permanently concluded. Sitting here in International House, he felt as though he had entered a tunnel and he was being forced to drive its length. He wanted only to leave it. All that prevented him from standing up and walking out of the bar, the building, the whole situation, was his desire to stand his ground in the presence of this obnoxious creature. Escape would come later. He burned with indignation.

Kate, for her part, showed almost no sign of strain, except to rapidly smoke one cigarette after another. Wayne continued to be sullen and vaguely hostile, asking several snide questions about crime magazines, but he seemed mainly interested in speaking with Kate. Eventually Mark stood up and said he would be waiting in the hall.

He paced back and forth next to the pub entrance, considering his options: He could leave; he could wait for Wayne to emerge and then jump him. It wasn't out of the question, a fight with this man. He might even win. But who *was* he? Who was this new antagonist? And what was the problem? It was too unattached to any context for Mark to act on his anger, but this only left him feeling helpless and ineffectual.

By the time Kate emerged a minute later he was in a fury.

"Listen, I'm so sorry about that," she said. "That was like Dr. Jekyll and Mr. Hyde. He's normally very well behaved."

Mark had already formulated a terse speech, calculated to do maximum emotional damage, and now he said his lines with the stilted quality of an actor reading from a script.

"All I can say," he began, "is that I hope that guy is either your current or recently ex-boyfriend, because if he's not then you must have some very melodramatic friends."

"He's not," she said, rolling her eyes. "That's the thing." She laughed as she said this, as though it was terribly amusing, and for the first time Mark saw that it was.

"He's not your boyfriend?" he said. They were walking down one of the low-ceilinged hallways of the building.

"No."

"Not your ex-boyfriend?"

"No."

He stopped walking and stared at her. "Then what the hell was that all about?"

"I don't know!"

"I mean, that was crazy!"

"I know!"

"You mean he's not your boyfriend, he's not anything, you didn't . . . you haven't . . ." And here a doorway out of the black heat of his indignity opened before him, and he gratefully stepped through it. "Jesus Christ, if I knew that I would have pulverized him!" he said. "I thought I had walked into some horrible emotional tangle. If I knew that I would have creamed him, I would have pounded his head into his shoulders." His voice took on a singsong, elated quality: "I would have mashed him, I would have crumpled him, I would have torn him to bits!" He let out a scream of completely inappropriate volume for indoors: "Ahhhhh! What an asshole!"

"Shhh, quiet," said Kate. "I know. It was so *weird*. I'm just

169

barely friends with this guy, and not even that until a few weeks ago, and he's acting like he . . . it's really upsetting." She didn't sound upset, though.

They walked hurriedly down the twisting hallways giggling in an elated conspiratorial manner and thoughtlessly holding hands. Eventually they pushed through a set of doors and emerged onto a large outdoor patio, home to a volleyball court, a couple of basketball hoops, and several benches. They sat down on one of them, close together, and listened to the street sounds drifting up from several floors below. International House rose up behind them, its hundreds of windows blinking like stars. The sky was clear but still hazy with warmth, and a silvery glow emanated from behind the building across the street.

"I don't even like to fight," said Mark when he had calmed down.

"That's good," said Kate.

"I think about it, but when it comes down to it, I just don't like to. Maybe I *should* like it. But I don't. It's the punched-in-the-face thing."

"I know," she said. "The whole thing was awful."

"Who wants to get punched in the face? For what? But I think about it, you know, sometimes I really just get going and start thinking about taking pliers and ripping someone's face off, you know?"

"Yeah, I know."

"You think about taking pliers and ripping someone's face off too?"

"Not exactly. I get really angry at people sometimes, though."

He was prepared to devote the next hour to careful analysis of what had happened in the bar, but Kate looked at him in a certain way, and his energy suddenly redirected. The opportunity surprised him. He rested his hand on her knee and squeezed lightly. She stroked his neck with her fingertips.

"Your heart is beating like crazy," she said. "I can feel it." Her eyes radiated affection. He nearly giggled at his sudden change in fortune.

"Are you always surrounded by this much drama?" he said.

"Sometimes," she said.

It was a wonderful thing, their first kiss, but not a complete success. After a few trial approaches, including one horrifying moment when they both turned their heads in the same direction and bumped noses, they pressed their mouths together and stayed like that for perhaps half a minute, until she pulled away.

"We're kind of in public," she said. Hundreds of windows glowed behind them. He could be in any one of them, Mark thought, watching. He quite enjoyed the idea.

The light behind the opposite building had gotten brighter, and then a thin splinter of bright silver appeared above the roof. They both turned towards it.

"Look," he said. "It's the moon."

They kissed some more, and Kate's thoughts drifted back and forth from what she was doing to the scene in the pub. She had not been entirely forthcoming with Mark—there had been one fleeting drunken episode with Wayne at a party several months earlier, when she had briefly given in to his advances and let him kiss her for a minute, maybe less. She had then pushed him away and explained that she didn't want to do that, and Wayne had been perfectly nice, even courtly, in the subsequent weeks and months. It was a nonevent, a tiny meaningless thing. But the evening's events had brought it back. It made her feel as if she had been in some kind of danger all these months, as though she had been using an old steamer trunk as a coffee table only to later find out it had a dead body in it.

She had been horrified by Wayne's behavior, but on some level it seemed in keeping with the strange bouts of hostility that men seemed to pass through without warning or logic. It was like weather. After months of keeping her distance, she had allowed herself to make friends with Wayne again after they discovered that they both smoked and jogged. Their friendship revolved almost entirely around running together. It was not romantic, but there was something coiled about Wayne; he was almost too polite at times.

Evidently the experience with Wayne had touched some chord of male anxiety in Mark, and on their breaks from kissing he went on about the problem with fighting.

"I've always thought of myself as a peaceful person, and I hardly ever get into fights," he said. "And yet there's something about me that seems to antagonize people. I don't even have to say anything. It's like a pheromone. They sense it."

"Aren't pheromones those chemicals that make animals immediately want to procreate? Like if a dog gives off pheromones all the other dogs in the neighborhood start to . . ."

"The thing is," he continued, too self-absorbed to pursue this other train of thought, "it's usually authority types. Gym teachers never liked me. I get near certain people and they're suddenly overcome with this strong desire to hit me. I can't decide if it's a good thing or not."

"It doesn't sound like a good thing."

"Well, it could mean that I have a special quality. But then it could mean that I'm just an irritating person, it's hard to say. It's not that this happens often. But I've noticed it. I get this strange energy from some guys."

"Me too."

"Is it violent?"

"No, but sometimes they get sort of strange and expectant, like I've done something to lead them on. Actually, men have been paying strange attention to me since I was about thirteen."

They kissed some more.

Eventually he suggested they visit her room, and she agreed. In the elevator she considered if her taking him up to her room at one in the morning might be suggestive in a way that she didn't quite intend, but she decided not to worry about it. Besides, in the course of the evening she had begun to like him quite a bit. She had already thought he was attractive, and seeing him all aflutter about this stupid confrontation provided a degree of emotional intimacy that weeks of dinners and movies would not have matched.

Mark had the same thought. They each contemplated their strange good fortune in silence until the door slid open.

He said he needed to go to the bathroom. She directed him down the hall and then pointed at the opposite end of the hall. "I'm the last door on the right," she said, and there they parted ways.

Her room contained a single bed, a desk, a bookshelf, and enough space to change clothes in. Its most redeeming feature was the window, which looked out onto the upper tiers of Riverside Church—Gothic, ornate, its pale white stone looming in the darkness. She considered neatening up, but sat on her bed instead and thought about Wayne.

All year he had been one of the many anonymous faces with whom she had exchanged polite nods of recognition; only in the last few months, after she had ended an affair with a boy on the seventh floor, had they become friends. And hadn't she been adamantly clear that her relationship with him was not and would never become anything more than friendly? She scoured her memory for a suggestive comment or gesture she might have recently made, but found nothing. She recalled a brief exchange they had had earlier in the evening, when she mentioned that she was meeting a man for drinks who worked at *Inside Detective* magazine. His reaction was to chuckle.

The whole thing made her nervous. Mark had inadvertently hit on a sensitive spot for her: her relationships with people did seem to be tinged with melodrama, particularly her relationships with men. A dark shadow of suspicion had begun to creep up within her that perhaps she was, if not responsible, then at least complicit, unable to see problems developing until they were too far gone. Maybe she was the same as Mark, she thought. Maybe it was pheromones.

The thought of Mark's anxious ruminations on why certain people were hostile to him made her smile, and it was with a smile on her face that she first heard the sound of men yelling in the hall. She opened her door and poked her head out just in time to see Mark, who was walking backwards, make an obscene gesture at Wayne, who was walking towards him saying, "What's the matter, tough guy? Come on, tough guy, you're a real big guy, you know that?"

Mark shouted some obscenities whose authority was somewhat undermined by the fact that he was backing up the whole time, and he nearly bumped into her as he backed through the door. He stepped past her and slammed the door shut.

"What the hell was that?" said Kate, and reached over to flip the lock. In the interval before he could answer, Wayne began pounding on the door. It shook. "Open the door," he yelled, his voice trembling with anger.

"Go away!" screamed Kate, "Leave us alone!" A moment later there was silence.

Mark immediately started to pace, but the room he had just entered allowed him to take only three steps in either direction.

"What's going on? What was that?" she said.

Mark didn't answer. He was in the midst of trying to loosen a knot that was taking up all the available space in his chest. The closeness he had felt towards Kate a few minutes earlier was gone now, as was every other emotion not bound up in the knot.

"What was that?" said Kate again. "Talk to me."

"Just give me a minute," said Mark, and continued to pace.

"Will you please stop pacing please!" She was now sitting on the bed, knees pulled up to her chest, and this allowed Mark an extra step in each direction. The knot began to loosen, and so he was able to speak.

"Jesus Fucking Christ," he said, and then, "Fucking Jesus Christ," and then, "Fucking Jesus Fuck," and then finally, with a deep sigh that did more than anything to loosen the knot, "God!"

"What's going on?"

"That guy is a maniac."

175

"What happened?"

"Nothing! I mean, nothing logical. I went into the bathroom and there he is, standing at the sink taking his contact lenses out. So I go, 'Ahhhh.' "

"What does 'Ahhhh' mean?"

" 'Ahhh' means 'Look who we have here,' or it means 'It's you again,' or it's a sort of shorter more polite version of 'Ahhh, shit.' In any case, I went over to take a piss, but the body is wiser than the mind in these instances, and knows that when left alone in a room with a psychotic orangutan it's best if you're not in the midst of peeing when he jumps on your back."

"Did he jump on your back?"

"No, but there seemed to be the threat of it. So I was just standing there in this deathly silence. I don't know what it's like for women, but for a guy the most thunderous silence in the world is when you're standing there trying to pee and . . ." His voice cracked at this moment, and he realized that he was quite upset. He took several deep breaths in the silence of the room and fought it off. It was intensely embarrassing.

"And if you're trying to pee and someone else is in the room, and nothing is happening, it's sort of a horrible situation. So there I was, in the midst of this humiliating silence, and he says to me . . . What's up with this guy, anyway? Are you sure nothing was going on with you two?"

"What did he say?"

"He says . . . and I can't believe how corny this is, he must be reading the John Wayne Manual of Provocative Insults . . ."

"Will you get to the point and tell me what he said!"

He finally stopped pacing and looked at her. At precisely the moment when the knot in his chest seemed to have come undone, Kate had become upset. He could see it around her eyes and mouth. Her normally fine features were bunched together like the palm of a hand cupped for water. For the first time since he entered the room it occurred to him that all this was difficult for her too, that it was, in some odd way, an attack against her, by proxy. He sat down next to her on the bed.

"What he said, in a very hostile tone of voice, was: 'Are you gonna be long?' "

"He wanted to know if you would be peeing for a long time?"

Kate said this with such sincerity that he almost burst out laughing. Seeing her upset had an immensely consoling effect on him.

"No, I think he meant would I be long with you. And I said, 'You never know.' I wasn't clear on what was happening, and I was too busy trying to zip up my pants to think about it, since it was obvious I wasn't going to the bathroom anytime soon. And then he said, in this ridiculous tone of voice, 'Make it quick.' I mean, who *is* this guy? 'Make it quick'? 'Make it *quick*'? And at this point, I'm leaving. I'm, like, out the door, and he says, 'You know what? You're a fag.' I mean, he's really an artist, this guy, a real innovator. I'm like, 'Right, anything you say,' or something like that, I hardly remember, I was so freaked out by the level of hostility this guy was directing at me, I mean, he was furious, absolutely furious, I could hear it in his voice, and I don't even *know* the guy. Who *is* he? So he follows me out into the hall calling me a fag and so forth, and in the hall I turn to him and take my hand and put it down there and say, 'Suck on this.' Not the height of diplomacy, I know, but one's options are limited in these situations. And his response to this is to kick at me. A kick! A real sophisticated martial-arts Bruce Lee–style kick. He was about five feet away, so it was really a demonstration more than anything else, but at this point it's quite clear, this guy wants to have a fight. And then he brandishes a screwdriver at me—"

"He had a screwdriver in the bathroom?" Kate asked, looking concerned in the manner of someone wanting to get all the facts straight.

"It was one of those tiny screwdrivers you use to adjust your glasses. But he sort of waved it at me. And I'm thinking, all right, you can't just let yourself be harassed by this raving lunatic, fight back, be a man! But then I'm also like, who *is* this guy? I don't even know him. I'm going to fight some guy I don't even know just because some of his sexually frustrated psychotic sewage has splashed up against me? But then I'm like, what am I, a pussy?" He hesitated here and shot Kate a nervous glance. "I mean, so to speak. I mean, you know, there are certain expectations of what you're supposed to do. But what if I get hurt? I mean, which is more humiliating, to walk away from a fight, or stand up to somebody and maybe get punched in the face? For what? And then there is you. I mean, think about it, there is choice one, or choice two. It's like *Let's Make a Deal*. Behind Curtain One is a fight with an insane black belt over God knows what, and behind Curtain Two is this woman with whom I'm suddenly getting along really well waiting for me in her room. What would you do?"

"I don't believe this," she said, and pressed her hand against her forehead. "What happened then?"

"So I kept backing up and he kept calling me a fag and saying things like 'You're a real tough guy,' " very sarcastically, and then I got to your door. And that's what happened."

There was a period of silence after that, and Mark stood up, preparing to pace again, because the knot in his chest had begun to tighten as he recounted the story.

"Sit down," said Kate.

He sat down. They looked at each other. "I heard the last part," she said, almost whispering. It occurred to him that the facts of the matter had come to her through a third party, that she had not experienced these facts firsthand, as he had, and that she could potentially doubt his version of events. For a moment the knot clenched to a suffocating tightness, but then dissolved entirely. She seemed as though she might cry. He hesitated a moment, and then leaned forward and put his arms around her, and she put her arms around him.

"I'm so sorry," she whispered in his ear.

"It's not your fault," he whispered back.

"But it's so awful."

He didn't reply, because at that moment he was engaged in an embrace that was the exact opposite of awful. It was an embrace that was intensely sexual precisely because there was no overt sexuality in it; unlike their earlier embrace there was no kissing, no tentative explorations of areas that were adjacent to other, more sensitive areas. There was no flirtation or approximation to this embrace, no hidden agenda, just *it*—succor in its pure undiluted form. Only the hands moved, making slow caressing circles, like tendrils swaying in the summer breeze.

They stayed that way for a long time. At first Mark was lost in its depth, its texture and fragrance, the warm enveloping softness that was in such contrast to the hardness he had just experienced. And then his thoughts drifted to Wayne. He decided that what made him so unpleasant wasn't just the sheer hostility he expressed, but the pitifully naked jealousy and frustration that propelled it. The irrationality of it all seemed to contain a veiled threat to the world: First I'm gonna attack this one stupid guy, and if that doesn't work, I'm going to blow the whole place up! Mark could, on some level, relate to this. Hate and empathy clashed within him. He should have fought back, he thought, regardless of his opponent's motives, and the fact that he hadn't was a humiliation. Hate won. Without a single thing changing in his immediate environment, he was suddenly possessed of a single desire: revenge.

What could be done? All the options seemed either too violent or too petty. Bang him on the head with a baseball bat? Or go to the police. The latter had some allure. Law students had to go through a character review before they joined the bar; any criminal record would be most inconvenient. But this was too obvious, and too simple. He wanted something more effective, something memorable, something that would humiliate Wayne. And no sooner had the wish been stated that he thought: I'll fuck her. I'll fuck her, and when I come I will let out a groan so loud it will carry down the hall and jolt the bastard awake. It'll be worse than a nightmare.

The whole situation had unexpectedly turned from something confused and messy into something clear and orderly, and this made sense to him. He had a theory about situations like these: out of the least opportune moments came the best opportunities. Things happen when they are least likely to happen. Out of this miserable night would come a wonderful satisfaction. It was, he knew, a horrible thought, and he took great pleasure in it.

While Mark was delivering his explanation of what had happened in the hall, Kate had felt her strength slowly dissipate.

Things had stopped making sense, and irrationality exhausted her. In view of what the evening had come to, she felt that she had two choices before her: she could either get incredibly upset, or she could fall into Mark's arms. The choice was simple—she got incredibly upset. She buried her face in her hands and barely refrained from weeping. She thought of Wayne and the sound of his fists pounding on the door. She wondered if Mark had told her the truth. She had witnessed the beginnings of Wayne's bad behavior, but not its full flowering. On some level she doubted Mark—there was too much about the situation as he explained it that didn't make sense—but the implications of this just made things worse. She wanted very much to trust him, but if he was innocent of provoking Wayne, then who was guilty?

Then Mark put his arms around her, and this was much better. He began kissing her with a great deal of ardor. She experienced the pleasing shock of someone else's physical proximity, his heat. They held each other for a while, and progressed from there. Both of them had been pushed into an unusually heightened state by the evening's events, and as a result there was a vaguely panicked quality to the way their hands ran underneath shirts and in between thighs. His breathing took on a different quality which she recognized as the focused concentration of a man moving towards a very specific place between her legs. She heard faint sounds begin to emanate from his throat and chest, distant rumblings that she imagined would blossom into full-scale groans, obscene and aggressive, once he had gotten to where he was so intent on going. It would be disgusting. She liked the idea.

She pulled away and looked at him with a mixture of curiosity and revulsion. He appeared to be possessed of an animal desire that had nothing to do with her; she was its object, that was all. She had been with men who were thinking of someone else while they were fucking her; and she had been with men who were completely with her when she was thinking of someone else. It could be sexy or depressing, or both, and now, with Mark bearing down upon her, she contemplated whether to go ahead.

She let him pull her shirt off and unbuttoned her shorts. She wanted to fuck him. She reached under his shirt and felt a pronounced bit of softness around his hips and stomach, which she found surprising. Her hand moved up to the tight hardness of his chest and stayed there. She felt his heart beating. Then she didn't want to fuck him. His eager heart was strangely animal, impersonal. She squirmed beneath him, pressing her hands against his shoulders and pushing him away. He moved down and kissed her stomach and its general vicinity for some time. Then he was spreading her legs with his hands. His earnestness was amusing. She liked the idea again. He moved up on top of her and she felt something against her stomach, a hot object that belonged to neither of them, an independent entity. It lay wedged between them. Then a flash of panic passed through her body as he pressed himself against her. Then she didn't like the idea. Not at all. She tried to find the breath to say "Stop," but couldn't. His grip tightened around her thighs as he pressed them apart. Then she really didn't want to.

Then the phone rang. It was thunderous. It seemed to go on for a minute, and then silence. They both froze.

"I should get that," she said.

"Are you sure?" he replied, and, as if in answer, the ring came again.

Lying there on Kate's bed, seeing her naked body in full for the first time as she bent forward to reach for the phone, he thought, for no logical reason, that it was the building security on the phone making sure all was well, documenting the presence of a madman in the hall, announcing that he had been taken away. After about thirty seconds of conversation, he briefly entertained the notion that it was a friend or relative calling with somber news.

But finally it became clear who it was—it was *him*. She sat huddled at the end of the bed, wrapped in a towel, talking to him and, even worse, listening to him. She hardly said a thing, implying a monologue of heroic proportions at the other end of the line. She caressed his ankle while she listened, and he lay there, happy to be caressed but increasingly annoyed at his suddenly diminished role in the room. He wanted to get up, but didn't want to move his ankle, which seemed like an increasingly frail conduit to their activity of moments ago.

"Honey," he whispered, "get off the phone."

She stayed on. A minute went by. She took her hand away. He put his underwear on and sat cross-legged on the bed.

"Honey," he hissed. "Get off the *phone*."

Another minute. He only got short snippets: "Well then why . . ." "So that doesn't mean you have to . . ." "I know, I know that, but . . ."

At last he hissed: *"Will you get off the phone with that asshole!"* His eyes bulged with exasperation, his body jerked like a marionette. Then he realized how he must sound, how concealing, how desperate—the last-ditch effort of the conman trying to keep the game afloat, even when the game is up. He was conducting his case incorrectly, he realized, but the fact that there was a case at all meant he had somehow lost, and that the events of the evening were now open to interpretation. Everyone was now the agent of their own agenda, and his claim on the truth was no more valid than anyone else's.

He got dressed and decided that it would be a fairly safe time to go to the bathroom. He stepped into the hall and heard the faint murmur of Kate's voice behind him.

As he moved down the hall her voice faded, and another became audible, as though he were slowly turning the dial of a radio from one station to the next. He paused beside the door where the voice was loudest and listened. It was smoother and calmer than he remembered it. It was placating. It was intimate. He heard only a fragment before stepping into the bathroom, but it was to haunt him.

"Yes, I know, I know, but let me ask you this, *why would I* . . ." And then the door to the men's room closed behind him and the voice was gone. He shivered at the effectiveness of the rhetorical question. If it was left to her to piece out the logic of the evening, she would fail to. There was no logic. It's when things don't make sense that lies become most plausible. He took his time, stretched, washed his face, and walked briskly back to her room.

She had just hung up when he walked in.

"I don't know what to think," she said. "According to him . . ."

"I don't care what he said. If you can't see the situation for what it is, then there's really nothing to say."

"What exactly is the situation?" she said.

"Two people living on separate planets is how I would put it."

They sat in silence on the bed for a few moments. Soon he

would be out in the open air again, in the city, in the world as it really was. He longed for it. He hated her with a passion that surprised him.

A tiny pulse of desire moved through Kate just then; it wasn't physical, she just wanted clarity and a certain warmth, and she looked at Mark to see if she might find it. She looked into his eyes and saw a tangle of complications and conflicting emotions, a dense insoluble knot.

"It's just so hard to know what happened," she said.

Half an hour later, after much furious muttering on Broadway and frantic deliberation, Mark was marching through Harlem—whose streets were frighteningly, fantastically alive with activity at two in the morning—on his way to the 26th Precinct. He had seen Harlem from a car, from a bus, from a plane, but he had rarely set foot in it, and never at night, and now he walked through it with the nervous exhilaration of someone walking on coals and finding it doesn't hurt.

At the 26th Precinct, out of sheer exasperation, he filed a complaint with the on-duty officer, a middle-aged black man who sat behind his desk with the complacent and slightly fatigued quality of someone who had just eaten a huge hero sandwich. "I would like to report a crime," said Mark. The officer looked him up and down with some skepticism, as though looking for blood, and then pulled a form out of a drawer and turned on an ancient electric typewriter. He read off a checklist of questions: name, address, location of the incident, nature of crime, description of assailant.

"Was there a weapon?" he asked.

Mark paused for a moment before answering, "Yes." Asked

to specify the weapon, he said, "A tiny screwdriver." The duty officer—haggard, experienced, inured to every brutality—peered at him over the top of his glasses for a moment before typing it in. He pronounced each word as he typed: "A . . . tiny . . . screwdriver." Fifteen minutes later, three detectives—large burly men with their shirt buttons straining at the stomach and heavy black revolvers strapped to their belts—attended to him with the solicitous interest of doctors examining a patient with a rare disease. They asked him again and again, in mock deadpan seriousness, "Are you absolutely sure the weapon was a tiny screwdriver? Are you sure it was *tiny?*"

At this moment he had a vision of Riley. If ever there was evidence of the declining quality of crime, this was it. Oh, how Riley would have wailed in disgust if he could have seen this! "It's all lawsuits," he always groused, and what was this but another irrelevance, another drop in the ocean of pettiness that was swamping the world?

But how small were the evening's crimes? There was dumb and impulsive aggression: a misdemeanor. There was cowardice: another misdemeanor. But what about the truth? he thought. My version of the truth has been kicked in the head with a steel-toed boot! A felony! But what is the proper response to an Assault on Truth?

Sitting amidst the heft of the police officers, feeling the solidity of their bodies, the guns strapped on as though appendages, he considered the maze of half-truths and mixed motives that had propelled him through the evening and left him here, sitting in a wooden chair under fluorescent lights like a corrupt expert witness paid off to hold up a tiny screwdriver and insist it could be lethal.

What was his claim to truth, anyway? How dear was the truth when it stood in the way of what he wanted? Wasn't his desire for Kate corrupted by his ulterior motives? But then is one ever without ulterior motives, even when they are tiny, no more substantial than a grain of sand? And aren't those tiny grains—deceit, artifice, manipulation, seduction—the foundation on which everything else is built? Is that why love is so precarious?

He walked home with a small slip of paper documenting his complaint lodged in his pocket. The whole event had been boiled down to a number, and he would have to wave this number before various parts of the police bureaucracy for his complaint to move forward. The air had cooled magnificently, and he moved through it taking deep breaths, turning the small square of paper over in his pocket as he walked. Halfway home he threw it out.

LIVE WIRES

THE LIVING ROOM is quiet and serene, and Alex Fader takes a deep breath, as if the silence were a fragrance. Then the doorbell rings. He stands up and goes to answer it, wondering which guests have arrived first and feeling slightly annoyed at them for being on time. He makes strange and dramatic faces as he walks to the door; he has just shaved, and his skin has the texture of Plexiglas. He puts his hand on the cool doorknob, makes one last face, and catches a glimpse of himself in the hallway mirror. "Electrocution," he says, and flings the door open.

"Hi!" he nearly shrieks. "It's the Brienfields!"

"Hell-oo, Alexander!" cry the Brienfields and begin to pile into the apartment, crowded together under the weight of their winter coats and scarves and gloves, and a big shopping bag that contains the gifts. They see the empty living room and exclaim, "We're first!" with a hint of dismay.

Alex stares into the hearty, broad face of Mr. Brienfield. It is the face he has been greeting at this Hanukkah party for the past fourteen years, but this time it seems a little different; it's as though the blood behind Mr. Brienfield's cheeks has thinned somewhat, while the brow that sits like a ridge above his eyes has thickened. At twenty-five, Alex has begun to see his mother's friends in a new light.

"Here, give me everything," he says. "I'm the coat check." Years of practice have made Alex an expert on getting people to part with their coats. He heads down the long, dark hallway in the direction of his mother's room, where the bed is the designated resting spot for coats.

"Mom!" he whispers at the closed door to the dressing room. "People are here!"

Hurrying back to the living room, he tries to think of something to say to the Brienfields. Their relation to him, like that of so many of the people who come to the party, is no longer definable—they're just there, a fixed part of the landscape of affiliations and friends of the Fader family, that sprawling brood of two.

The doorbell rings again, and then he hears the metallic click of the door opening. Panic touches him. What if it's Christine? he thinks, and then, What could Christine and the Brienfields possibly talk about? What in the world was I thinking when I invited her to this thing? He enters the foyer just as the Zuckermans come walking in. Some private moment of truth has been postponed, and Alex smiles like a slot-machine player who has just won small. He likes the Zuckermans, as a family and individually. The parents are handsome, successful, and reserved, and the kids are appealingly bashful.

"Come in, come in, come in!" says Alex, and he presses hands and kisses cheeks. A damp coldness still hangs on the Zuckermans' coats; they live just four blocks up Riverside Drive and have walked. "Give me all your stuff. My mother—"

But just then their faces turn together and brighten as if an angel had appeared. Alex turns and sees his mother entering the foyer in a white silk shirt and billowy black pants; her clothes undulate with each step, giving her the appearance not so much of walking as of floating. Her face has the special glow and charm it takes on when she is anticipating the company of people she likes. The Brienfields and Zuckermans all move toward her instinctively, and Alex feels like an unmoving pier deserted by an outgoing tide.

His mother's translucent happiness provokes in him a mixture of elation and disgust. Watching her now, he's reminded of Anna Karenina. He has been reading the book for the first time since high school, and he has come to see more and more of his mother in the character of Anna. For one thing, the two women share a glowing and unaffected manner that people are drawn to. That, and a maddening willfulness. Watching his mother now, Alex thinks, It's a bitch having a mother who belongs to the nineteenth century.

The Zuckermans descend on her with cries of joy, mouths pucker into kisses, and fingers clasp necks and caress cheeks. The doorbell rings again, and Alex flees down the dark hallway with another armload of coats. The annual Fader Hanukkah party is officially under way.

The house has become crowded, and Alex moves from room to room, past people standing in little circles, as if around campfires. He doesn't join in the conversations yet, but pauses next to each one just long enough to get its flavor. There is something odd and exhilarating about having so many lives suddenly packed within walls that are used to so few. When he was a boy, he would become delighted and intimidated by this transformation to such a degree that he had to take breaks in his mother's room, burying his face among the coats and breathing the musty personal scent of dried rain and old perfume. Now he continues to roam, taking in the bright faces. He doesn't live here anymore, but in a way he does. But he doesn't.

He finds his mother in the kitchen, slicing cherry tomatoes into a huge wooden salad bowl. He comes up next to her and watches as the sharp blade presses against the red flesh of each tomato, penetrates it after encountering some resistance, and then quickly moves through it, miraculously stopping just as it reaches her thumb.

"How's it going?" he says.

"Oh!" she says, startled. "Very good. I'm almost done."

"Everybody is asking for you," he says. "I keep hearing your name murmured here and there. It's like you're some greatly anticipated celebrity who hasn't arrived yet." He scowls as he says this, and his mother at once picks up his train of thought.

"Is Christine here yet?" she asks.

"No. Not yet. I don't even know why I invited her. She's not even Jewish."

"Alexander! That doesn't matter. Many people come here who aren't Jewish."

It's true. This is a carefully secular Hanukkah party, as usual. But if it doesn't matter, he feels like saying, why do we bother to celebrate Hanukkah or Passover, or ever debate fasting on Yom Kippur? But he knows the answer—or rather, he doesn't know the answer but somehow understands it.

"Well, I imagine she's probably late because she's terrified," he says. "I described the goings-on here and I think I saw her cringe when I mentioned the singing."

"She'll enjoy it," says his mother, finishing with the last to-mato. "She's open-minded."

Alex feels a stab of irritation at his mother for presuming things about his girlfriend, though what she says about Christine is probably right. The two have met several times, and although their styles could not be more different, the two of them have seemed to connect. Alex has been intensely sensitive to the progress of these encounters. Christine is eight years older than he and occupies a strange place in the age spectrum, somewhere between himself and his mother. This worries him, for some reason.

"Come," says his mother. "Let's go out to the party." They step shyly into the foyer, pausing together to survey the scene. Then someone rushes up to Alex's mother with outstretched arms.

"Eve!" the woman cries. "Eve, hi. My God, I was wondering if I was going to see you at your own party!"

The woman is quite tall and thin, and her arms wrap around his mother like a lasso. She is one of the guests who show up each year whose names Alex can never remember. Last December, he discovered that she was a criminal judge, and as he watches her embrace his mother now, he tries to contrast the image with one of her sitting on the bench, meting out stiff sentences.

Alex drifts away, noticing details in their apartment—a small violin case, dust-covered, that sits under the piano, an antique dagger hanging on the wall—that he never notices unless other people are present. It's as if each object projects light.

Later on, with the party now in full swing, Alex is talking to one of his mother's old friends, Mrs. Talman. She has been dear

192

to him ever since they first met, when he was about eleven and she had pressed his head into her warm, plentiful, and highly fragrant breasts, in a polite but enveloping embrace. Now that he is grown up, it is her head that seems about to be pressed into his chest, but he still feels a charge whenever they are together. She has glittering, dark eyes and tan, Mediterranean skin.

"Look at this handsome man," she says. "I hear that your girlfriend is going to be here. I can't wait to meet her."

"Why?" says Alex defensively.

"Because she's your girlfriend. I'm curious to see what kind of company you're keeping." Noticing the distressed look on his face, she adds, "The advance word has been very favorable."

"I'm not quite sure why I invited her. I think I figured that if I didn't, it would be like hiding something from her."

"Or from us."

"The things I've been hiding from my mother and her friends could fill a textbook."

"I don't know about that," says Mrs. Talman. "Children always overestimate the naiveté of their parents. When it comes down to it, our secrets are much more shocking than yours."

It is into this atmosphere that Alex's current girlfriend and passionate flame, Christine Perry, steps gingerly. Alarm overtakes him as he sees her standing in the vestibule, looking into the mass of chatting guests with the expression of someone on a high diving board peering at the pool below.

"Oh, my God," he says out loud, as though a fire had just broken out. He glances apologetically at Mrs. Talman and rushes toward Christine. All his rationalizations for her presence crumble in the face of disaster. What is it about her at this party that makes him so uneasy? He has been putting the question to himself, and his answers feel insufficient. He and she have come from separate backgrounds—hers suburban and Midwestern—and now at this party his own background has been laid bare in all its foreignness. And then there is the difference in their ages. She is eight years older than he, a detail that would be undetectable—she has youthful features and fine, unlined skin—except that her hair, which is cut short to just below her ears, is unabashedly, almost defiantly, gray. None of this has proved to be an obstacle during their year together—in fact, these differences have made their closeness all the more exciting—but now it worries him.

As he approaches Christine, he feels a strong pulse of sensations he remembers from their first meeting. In their first conversation, at a another party, she had gazed at him impassively with her wide gray-blue eyes, with her center of gravity fixed with such calm precision that she hardly shifted her weight as they talked. A wave of anger had overtaken him. She seemed to be speaking to him from within a glass case, and he wanted nothing more than to shatter the glass. What he had ended up shattering was his plastic wineglass, which he had massaged with increasing force until it cracked and spilled his drink all over their shoes. It was during the ensuing laughter (hers) and stammered apologies (his) that they first connected.

His subsequent familiarity with the details of her life—her job at an advertising agency, her fussy insistence about drinking tea with enormous amounts of honey first thing in the morning, her lamentations about a jury summons—had slightly lessened his wish to shatter something, and with this change came an almost gallant protectiveness.

"You're late," he begins to say, but then catches himself. "It's our guest of honor!" he says instead.

"Hi," she says. "It's crowded."

He bends over and brings his face near hers. They've gotten into the habit of greeting each other by brushing the tips of their noses.

"I'd have been here sooner," she says, "but two pigeons landed on my windowsill and were going through this feverish courtship."

"I didn't know pigeons made out in December," Alex says. He is frowning. "Let me take your coat. It's my big job here, coat check. I've developed a talent for it."

"I don't know anyone," she says.

"What were you expecting? These are friendly old Jewish people."

He doesn't know why he said the word "Jewish," except perhaps to get it out of the way. He has never had an affair with a Jewish girl. It hasn't been a conscious decision, but it has become a noticeable fact.

"I'll introduce you to some people. I've been told that your arrival is greatly anticipated."

"By whom?"

"I don't know, exactly. I guess a lot of these people have known me since I was little, and they're curious to know what kind of company I'm keeping."

"They'll be horrified to know you're dating an old hag."

As she says this she slips out of her coat. It is a big gray woolen thing, and her body emerges from it like the tender insides of an enormous nut. Her dress is pink, her arms bare. She looks like candy, he thinks.

"I'll be right back," he says.

He hurries down the hallway with her coat, throws it on the bed, and is about to hurry back when the bed catches his eye. It is piled high with voluptuous winter coats, and a tremendous urge to take a swan dive into the pile comes over him. He pauses, debating it, and then remembers that his last such dive onto the bed, at age thirteen, had produced a sharp cracking sound, after which there was always a sag in one part of the bed. In any case, he's a grown-up now.

When Alex returns to the foyer, Christine is gone. A quick scan locates her at the other side of the room, with a woman named Julia. She is a nice lady who has been coming to the Hanukkah party year after year. She is one of several women who show up alone at these parties; they occupy an age somewhere between the mid-forties and mid-sixties, and have an upbeat but somewhat beleaguered quality. Alex has always looked at them with a mixture of curiosity and trepidation, the way someone waiting in line to go into a haunted house looks at the people just emerging, the better to gauge the effect of what lies within. These are women—there are a few men who come alone, too, but they are different—who have wound their way through love and marriage and children and divorce, and even death, and now, he sees, find themselves blinking outside in the daylight, alone. It's strange to think that this is a group that his mother belongs to, as well, though somehow she doesn't have that blinking quality.

Alex arrives in time to hear Julia say to Christine, "Really. I'm serious. Like in those trashy romance novels, you know, when they describe the heroine's skin—you know: smooth, white, porcelain, fair, twenty adjectives in a row—they're describing your skin. Really. I know. I wrote one."

"That's nice of you," said Christine. "I don't think I believe you, though."

Alex flashes to an image of Christine stepping into their bed with several layers of expensive and mysterious creams and mists massaged into her face. The process, which they jokingly refer to as "the Beauty Ritual," is so elaborate that it is a struggle for Alex to stay awake through it, and often he is awakened by Christine's body, in her pink pajamas, sliding into bed next to him.

"Hello, Alex," says Julia distractedly. "I was just telling your friend that she has exactly the kind of—"

"She thinks I look like one of those women in trashy books who are innocent and pure and end up sleeping with terrible men," says Christine.

"That's not quite how I put it," says Julia. She is about to elaborate when a shushing sound sweeps through the room and attention moves to the baby grand piano in one corner of the room, behind which stands his mother.

"Everybody," she says, "it's time for the singing. Those who know how it goes, and there should be many of you by now, please sing along, and those who are new, there are sheets being passed around."

Guests arrive from all parts of the apartment, crowding into the living room and bearing chairs and drinks, and now fumbling with the song sheets.

Alex looks at Christine with an apologetic expression. "Does this seem really weird?" he says.

"No," she says. "It seems nice."

Her answer doesn't quell his anxiety, but he is called over to the piano. It is time for the lighting of the candles. People sit in chairs pressed up close to one another, making an unruly semicircle around the piano. Four unfortunate guests are perched on the remains of the couch, which is elegant in its external appearance, a few rips aside, but otherwise completely ruined. Anyone sitting down on it, Alex knows, is sucked down into a swirl of cushions and springs, and practically lowered to the floor. He stares at two couples lined up there, each person trying to act as if the awkward position they've been placed in—knees up near their armpits—is not unusual. He vows not to make a nervous joke about the couch. He has made a joke about it every year for as long as he can remember. Then, with the oily loquaciousness of a lounge-act m.c., he murmurs, "Um, if anyone is missing a friend, you might want to check the couch. It's a lovely couch but it's relation to furniture is similar to the Venus flytrap's relation to flowers."

Then the matches are handed to him. Silence. A little red-tipped twig in his fingers. The thunderous crack of the tip against the brown flint of the matchbook. Success, on the very first try. And then the horrible, aching, off-key sound of his own voice half chanting, half singing, as he lights the middle candle and then passes its flame from candle to candle. It is the last night of Hanukkah, so all eight candles have to be lit, and he tries to get each wick going as soon as possible. *"Baruch ata adonai eloheinu melech haolam,"* he croaks. *"Asher kidshanu bemitzvotav . . ."* He manages to sing with a moderate amount of vigor, telling himself that his religion seems to stipulate that such songs be sung in an off-key, wavering voice, with hardly any sense of rhythm.

When it is over he joins his mother on the piano stool, and the room stumbles its way through the first song, his mother almost the only one to sing the words with a clear, melodic voice. At the end Alex feels a huge sense of relief mingled with regret. Everyone, he has noticed, feels uncomfortable with the singing until the last note has begun to fade, at which point everyone pretends to have enjoyed it all. It's Hanukkah. The pile of gifts under the menorah looms large, and appetizing smells waft in from the kitchen.

"Very good!" his mother calls out when the last mooing, mumbling words have died away. "Let's try that one again!"

Alex feels the room's collective heart sink, and he bends his head so as not to have to look at anyone. The guests launch into it again, and a few more voices join in: *"Maoz Tsur yeshuati . . ."* When it's over, his mother plays another, slightly more lively song. And then finally a last, peppy one.

"This one is called 'Svevivon,' " she says, "and it's about a little dreidel which is very mischievous and runs through the woods and the streams and goes anywhere it wants." The words "woods and streams" seem almost criminal to Alex. They belong to a pre-ironic language that the world has long since cast aside. His mother starts to play. He stares at her fingers on the white and black keys. They aren't the world's most elegant fingers, yet they exude the maddening kind of optimism possessed by people who like to plant gardens. The lyrics of this last song are repetitive, and more and more people gradually join in. His mother quickens the pace, and without stopping spins the song into a second go-around. For a moment Alex lets his eyes flicker upward. He sees a tableau of faces, some somber, some cheerful, some staring with concentration down at individual sheets of paper while they sing, some singing heartily to the ceiling, some outright faking it. He half glimpses Christine, sitting in one corner, and can't tell if her lips are moving.

All the faces are bathed in a warm light from the lamps around the room; some of the silk lampshades, he knows, are ripped on the inside, and fringes of silk hang down like vines;

others are so old that they cast off a yellow glow, like a candle's. The moment seems to contain everything about life that is attractive and perfect and nourishing and also everything that makes one want to flee and hide under a rock and hope that someone someday might find a cure for—for the awkward, transparent fragility of people such as these.

It is over. Gifts are distributed—a surfeit of scarves for the men, more personal things for the women—and then everyone begins to file into the study for dinner: a buffet. Alex finds Christine talking to Mrs. Zuckerman. He catches Christine's eye but then decides to leave her alone. She and Mrs. Zuckerman seem relaxed together. A sense of lightness comes over him, now that the main event is over. Finally relinquishing her duties, his mother is roaming around, talking to people, and Alex keeps shifting his gaze from Christine to his mother and back. They're like two live wires, separate yet each connected to him. He is aware of an impulse to keep them apart, but doesn't know what it means.

The party starts to wind down—a gradual thinning and then a sudden rush. Then it is done. The last people crowd down the hallway in a group, holding their coats and gifts. There is an awkward period in the hall, while the elevator climbs and slows, and everyone's attention turns to the churning, wheezing sounds it makes as it prepares to stop. They huddle in, offer a last, frantic flurry of waves and goodbyes as if they were on the deck of a departing ship, and the door closes.

Alex and his mother and Christine come back into the apartment, which is awash in ribbons and colored paper and scattered chairs and plates and half-emptied wineglasses with traces of lipstick around the edges. This moment, too, has duplicated itself year after year, though now there is a variation—the cast has grown to three.

Alex realizes that the most difficult part of the evening is at hand. It is a foregone conclusion that he's going home with Christine, but how he is going to negotiate the transition is suddenly a mystery.

"Oh my!" says his mother, exultant with relief. "That was one of the best ones." Then she turns to Christine. "Thank you so much for coming."

"Why are you thanking me? I should thank you. It was a really nice party. I've never been to a Hanukkah party before. It was amazingly friendly."

Once again, her calm assurance—the first thing he had ever noticed about her—strikes Alex. She is performing a social function with this sort of talk, but there is something about her, an openness, that takes it somewhere else. Her cheeks are full of color, and her eyes seem unusually bright.

"Shall we open the presents?" says his mother.

Alex stands still. The business of opening presents with his mother is so personal that he can't imagine this third party taking part. The two women look at him, and he is reminded of an unpleasant experience he had not long ago with his incoherent Aunt Louise, his father's sister, who lives in a nursing home in New Jersey. She has Alzheimer's. During the visit, he had waved a picture of Christine in front of her face and said, "This is my girlfriend. My *girlfriend*. What do you think? Not bad, huh?"

Aunt Louise rarely said anything, so Alex was in the habit of keeping up both sides of the conversation in her presence. But this time she swerved briefly back into the cantankerous and acerbic woman she had been for so many years, and her face took on an alarmed and vaguely contemptuous expression. "Eve," she said. "It's Eve."

"No, no," said Alex, horrified. "It's my—" But his aunt's eyes removed themselves again and he was left staring at the photograph, struck by the idea that he had managed to find a woman who resembled his mother when she was younger. He saw it quite suddenly: the same broad, smooth forehead, the pencil-thin eyebrows, the elegant nose. But most of all the mouth—that half-smile that was an expression neither of happiness nor sadness, coldness nor affection, but of a private and elusive pleasure.

Now, staring back at these two faces, he feels unsure of how best to proceed. He doesn't like the idea of the three of them opening gifts. Christine would tear hers open, and his mother would unpeel each piece of tape, to preserve the wrapping, and he would sit in the middle feeling embarrassed.

"I'll do the dishes," he suddenly offers. "There are all these dishes and I can't leave you with them. It's not fair. Let's just clean up first." For the first time in his life he is glad that his mother has never owned a dishwasher.

In moments, he is in his official dish-washing posture—his forehead pressed to the cabinet above the sink while his hands and arms work—and he enters a dish-washing trance. Christine and his mother move about the apartment, gathering dishes and glasses and silver and bringing them to him. Nearly an hour has passed by the time the last spoon has been rinsed and dried. Christine and his mother are sitting at the kitchen table, talking, their faces pleasant and relaxed.

"Well," Alex says finally. "I guess that's that."

"All right," says his mother. The air is filled with departure. Her face smiles brightly, but Alex can read something slightly forced about it. The gifts still lie unopened.

"I'll get our coats," he says and goes to retrieve them.

As he and Christine are leaving, Alex notices that the living room looks like a stage set after the play is over and the actors have all gone home. Chairs stand at odd angles from one another, and remnants of the party are scattered about. The menorah, which had presided grandly over the event, now sits quietly, its eight candles burnt down. The neat pile of unopened gifts that lies at its base—his gifts for his mother, hers for him, and those brought by the guests—seems like an oversight. The idea of his mother left alone on this stage is suddenly excruciating to him, and his departing manner is almost abrupt.

"All right, that was great," he says. "I'll call you tomorrow. We'll do the presents soon."

"Thank you so much, Eve," says Christine, and the sound of his mother's name on her lips surprises him. The two women embrace warmly, pausing in each other's arms almost as if in commiseration. He is entirely outside of this moment, and he peers at them curiously, wondering what is happening. They have more in common with each other than either has with him. Two women and a bystander. Then he bends to kiss his mother's warm cheek.

Out in the hall, a vague dizziness overtakes him as the dial beside the elevator slowly turns toward the number of their floor. The door opens. He and Christine step in. It closes behind them, his mother's face momentarily visible through the small rectangular window in the elevator door.

"Bye!" calls Christine.

The elevator starts down. "Goodbye," comes the reply, but his mother's face has disappeared.

It is a cold, clear winter night, and the streets are hard, wind-swept, and empty. Alex and Christine walk hand in hand to-ward West End Avenue, the sound of their shoes echoing against the pavement.

"What did you think?" Alex says after a minute.

"It was nice," Christine says. They walk in silence for few more steps. "There was something heartwarming about it. And sort of heartrending, too, the way all those people seemed so friendly and kind, and your mother being so enthusiastic. It's almost enough to make you optimistic about people."

"Almost," says Alex.

She says nothing more, and for a moment he hates her.

They wait on the deserted corner until an empty taxi screeches to a stop in front of them. They clamber in and head downtown towards Christine's apartment. It is an old taxi, with windows that don't quite close and ancient shocks. The smell is pleasant, though: old leather and some previous passenger's perfume. Alex and Christine huddle against each other in the backseat.

"Alex?" she says at one point.

"Yeah?" he replies, but she doesn't say anything else.

The cold wind whistles through the doors. Every block or so they hit a bump and the cab rises off the ground as though it had just flown over the crest of a hill. The glow of each passing streetlight falls across Christine's face and then recedes. Alex reflects on the impossibility of his relationship with her—the doom and despair that await him, and the heartbreak. He misses the familiar warmth and security of the apartment he has just left. Yet his departure has been inevitable—a thrilling turn of events. He holds Christine tight as they go over a bump. Up goes the taxi in a smooth, effortless glide, and a tiny smile comes over Alex's face as they hang in midair.

ACKNOWLEDGMENTS

I WOULD LIKE TO THANK *the following individuals and institutions for their support: Jerome Badanes, Mary Gaitskill, Roger Angell, Mary Evans, Gerald Howard, Robert Towers, Philip Lopate, Stephen Koch, Susan Minot, The Saint Ann's School, Yaddo, Marcelle Clements, William Gifford, Elizabeth Grove, Liselotte Bendix Stern, and Berta Beller.*